AM I BEING FOLLOWED?

AM I BEING FOLLOWED?

G. M. Hutchison

Matador
9 Priory Business Park,
Wistow Road, Kibworth Beauchamp,
Leicestershire. LE8 0RX
Tel: 0116 279 2299
Email: books@troubador.co.uk
Web: www.troubador.co.uk/matador
Twitter: @matadorbooks

ISBN 978 180046 323 3

British Library Cataloguing in Publication Data.
A catalogue record for this book is available from the British Library.

Printed and bound in Great Britain by 4edge Limited
Typeset in 11pt Jenson Pro by Troubador Publishing Ltd, Leicester, UK

Matador is an imprint of Troubador Publishing Ltd

chapter
one

I DREW INTO A LAY-BY AND REACHED FOR MY flask. Since this was the last time I would be making a journey such as this I didn't feel as nervous as I usually did.

I had known from the start that it was wrong to do work of this kind but, so far, my conscience hadn't bothered me very much. Instead, my main concern had been to make sure that I didn't get caught, or something like that. Caught by whom I wasn't sure but, whoever they were, I felt certain they posed a serious threat to my well-being. Not today, however. I could relax and listen to some music.

I couldn't decide which piece to play and before long I got bogged down thinking about what Pastor Mackenzie had said about the universe. It was the sun beginning to beat down on the car roof which had started me off on this, the fact that such a far-distant heavenly body could emit rays that were making me, here in this car, right now, feel uncomfortable. This undeniable fact certainly touched on some of the things he had said, in a very down-to-earth fashion. I didn't want to lower the window, however, because of the noise from the passing traffic.

With no fresh air to break my train of thought I continued mulling over some of the points the Pastor had made. The universe, according to him, with all its planets, stars and galaxies, declared forcefully to those who studied it with unblinkered eyes that God existed, was all powerful, and possessed an intelligence that bore a certain similarity to our own but was immeasurably superior to it. As did the oceans, too, with all the mysteries contained in their unfathomable depths, and not forgetting the dry land either, he would go on, with all its trees, shrubs, flowers and vegetation.

It was when he added man to his list that I began to part company with him. I thought it strange that someone like him, in the business of loving his fellow men, should seem to have such a low opinion of them and always be describing their limitations.

Man, with all the understanding he has gained from a study of nature, he would point out, is still in awe of the greater part of it and, with all his scientific prowess, can't even create the simplest of life forms. Nor, in all this breathtaking spectacle, he would frequently add, had there ever appeared naturally so much as one plant or animal that was in every respect the same as any of the others.

I wondered how he could have reached many of his pet conclusions without taking the opinions of the scientists fully into account. After all, Evolution was now confirmed in the text books. But this objection wouldn't do, I soon found out. Science was demonstrable fact, he would declare, whereas Evolution, strictly speaking, was only a theory often and quite wrongly used to elevate conjecture over proof. And anyway, as he would even more often assert, "Evolution, in certain respects, was probably part of The Divine Plan, too."

I wondered what he would think of me if he knew what I was doing right now. It would be putting it mildly to say that he wouldn't approve, although this wouldn't give rise to any real problems, I felt, since this would be the last run. I would be law-abiding again after this.

I glanced in the mirror and saw the driver of a car, which had drawn into the lay-by behind me, get out and walk round to the front of his vehicle. Emptying the contents of my flask into the cup, I tilted my head backward to ensure that the last dregs reached my mouth and, as I did so, someone tapped on the car window, a visitor whom I saw at once was the driver of the nearby car.

He was a well-built man, not much older than myself, I could see. He was clean-shaven and wore a well-cut leather jerkin. I lowered the window.

"Sorry to trouble you," he said, smiling and leaning in towards me. "Do you happen to have a spanner or a pair of pliers I could borrow?"

I laid the flask and the empty cup on the floor and, as I turned in my seat to get out of the car, the man stepped back and, to my horror, brought a small black handgun out of his trouser pocket.

"Give me the package," he ordered, pointing the weapon at me menacingly.

Although his features still showed traces of the polite, enquiring look they had at first worn, his smile seemed forced now and his eyes stared threateningly.

"The package," he repeated, in a harsher tone.

As I reached into the back of the car and brought the package over the seat onto my lap, he ordered me to get out of the car.

"Leave the package on the seat and go down to the boot," he snapped, motioning in that direction with his free hand.

As I walked towards the rear of the vehicle I half-turned and, out of the corner of my eye, saw him lay the package on the ground, steadying it with his foot as he tore at the wrapping.

"Get back in the car," he then ordered, gruffly gesturing with the gun.

As I sat down behind the steering wheel he stood outside, motionless, staring at me, one hand holding the torn package at his side, the other pointing the gun at me.

During most of the time on these trips my nerves had been on edge. Spasms of apprehension, anxiety and fear had surged through me continually as I had imagined the various dangers I might be facing. Now that the worst had happened, all I could feel was that I had done something wrong. What would Andy have done in these circumstances? I asked myself, looking for an excuse. Surely anyone, even Andy himself, having a gun pointed at them from close up like this, would have handed the package over as I had just done?

I watched the man go back to his car, throwing the package onto the passenger seat, before he settled behind the wheel and drove off.

I painfully realised just what I had done wrong as I watched the vehicle disappear into the distance. I wouldn't have lost the package so easily on the previous run, or on the very first one for that matter, I told myself. Keyed up and suspicious of every vehicle I encountered, I would have seen the arrival of another car in the lay-by as a threat. I would have driven off, therefore, as I am sure Andy would have done, too. Instead, I had sat dreamily in the car, drinking tea and thinking about the universe.

I felt annoyed at first that Andy hadn't warned me that something like this might happen. On the contrary, according to him, the deliveries were just an easy way of making money.

As an excuse this wasn't good enough, though, I soon realised. The very nature of the work had carried a risk without

Andy having to describe it. The plain fact was, I had slipped up, to say the least. I hadn't been smart enough. I shouldn't have stopped in the lay-by, or I should have driven off when the other car appeared. My brief excursion into Andy's world, I reflected dismally, had now proved as unsuccessful as most of my other ventures in life.

From the car park the Old Toll Bar didn't look very inviting. I felt the scene looked just about right on this occasion, aware of the contrast in being a bearer of bad news rather than a dispirited employee looking for succour in the warm and friendly atmosphere.

Karen was sitting at the usual table.

"I've been waiting for you", she told me, an unexpected note of urgency in her voice. "Let's go out to the car."

"Where's Andy?" I asked her. "I was supposed to meet him here."

Something else had gone wrong, I could see. She couldn't possibly know about what had happened to me and yet she looked every bit as keyed up as I was.

"Andy's hurt," she told me as we reached the car. "He sent me to find you."

"Hurt in what way?"

She turned to face me. She seemed to be annoyed at me, not just concerned about what had happened to Andy.

"He's been shot," she told me bluntly.

"Shot?" I gasped, not altogether surprised, in view of what had just happened to me.

"I had a feeling that something like this was going to happen," she muttered.

"Karen. Something like what?"

"You'd better ask Andy," she snapped at me. "He's at the caravan."

"Has he seen a doctor?"

"Of course he's seen a doctor," she said irritably.

I couldn't be blamed for what had happened to Andy, and I hadn't put a foot wrong in my relationship with her, either. Why was she annoyed at me?

"I thought you said you were only a courier?" she said accusingly.

"I am only a courier!" I protested.

"Andy gets shot and the first person he sends for is you," she said, staring at me angrily.

"Not exactly, Karen. He sent you to get me before that, didn't he?" I countered.

"Don't include me in the equation," she stated coldly. "I only work at the Casino. I work for a salary, and Andy doesn't write the cheque."

"I only do deliveries, Karen, if that's what you're getting at."

As the caravan park at last came into view, bringing relief from the added tension her attitude had generated, she slowed the car to a crawl and turned again to face me.

"Sorry, if I'm getting it wrong" she said quietly. "I jumped to the conclusion you'd been holding out on me and that you were part of the Operation."

"Definitely only as a courier," I reaffirmed in a gentler tone.

Andy was lying on the couch at the far end of the caravan. He sat up, wincing as he manoeuvred his heavily bandaged leg under the table.

"Andy, I've lost the package," I blurted out.

He slumped back despairingly against the pillow he had been using to prop himself up, and closed his eyes.

"Sorry, Andy. He had a gun," I added feebly.

"You've not been hurt, though?" he asked, coming to life and heaving himself back up into a sitting position.

I felt Karen's eyes on me as I gave Andy a description of what had happened to me and supposed this would bring about another change in her attitude, on this occasion probably because I hadn't confided in her on the way here.

"This is a right bloody mess," Andy said slowly, as if thinking out loud. "John, I'm sorry I got you involved in this."

"What actually happened?" I asked him impatiently. "Who shot you, Andy?"

"Steve."

"But I thought Steve was one of you," Karen said to him in apparent disbelief, echoing my own thoughts on the matter.

"Well he isn't," Andy replied stiffly. "Not that it matters now anyway", he went on. "He's got the package, which unfortunately means a lot more trouble all round, for all of us."

"Trouble of what kind, Andy?" I asked nervously.

He bit down on his lip, shaking his head despairingly. This was the first time I had seen Andy like this. He wasn't sure what to do.

"You mean they'll blame us?" Karen asked him, "regardless of what's actually happened?"

"It's not just a question of blame, Karen. I'm supposed to stop this kind of thing happening, not to become a victim."

"I mean, what's the bottom line, Andy?" I asked firmly. "And where does all this leave us?"

"We've become targets, John" he answered coldly. "It's not good. I don't know how it will all pan out."

This was what I had always felt uneasy about. I was no longer merely on the fringe of some vague criminal organisation, able to feel that I wasn't really a part of it. Whatever had gone seriously wrong for the Operation, had gone seriously wrong for me, too. What I had dreaded had materialised. I had been right to wonder what all this might lead to.

"So where does Steve fit in?" I asked. "If he's not part of the Operation, who exactly is he?"

The question seemed to annoy him, or was he just annoyed at me?

"I'm sorry about this Andy," I told him.

I thought again of the first run, when I had been suspicious of every car on the road. No-one could have crept up on me then.

"It wasn't really your fault, John. What else could you have done?"

Andy's words didn't help. Whether or not it was my fault wasn't the immediate issue anymore. I was now mixed up in something that was far too much for me. I wasn't just dabbling in it. I was a part of it.

"I had absolutely no idea that anyone was following me, Andy", I pleaded.

"I know you didn't, John", Andy said sympathetically. "Strictly speaking he didn't need to follow you, anyway. Steve would have told him the route."

"The last time I saw Steve, the shoe was on the other foot. It was him who didn't see me," I pointlessly remarked, remembering how I had spotted him when I had been driving on the coast road with Linda.

"What last time?"

"On the Shore Road, a few days ago, He was in one of the vans."

He glanced at Karen, as if what I had just told him was significant.

"Exactly where on the Shore Road?" he asked. "Bartons don't do much business out there, do they. It's too far out?"

"Bellsmore, it's called. I think he'd been in the caravan park."

"It's not likely, Andy." Karen cut in. "It's just a coincidence."

"What is?" I asked irritably. I might not be at the top of the pecking order, but I was in this now as much as they were.

"There's a caravan there that we once used as a safe house, but that particular route was discontinued," Andy explained. "Steve would have known all about this."

"It's too obvious," Karen commented dryly.

"Not in the short term it isn't," Andy reasoned. "They would have to meet up somewhere, wouldn't they?"

"I suppose so," she nodded grimly. "What does it matter anyway?"

"They could still be there, couldn't they? They'll think they're in the clear," Andy pointed out.

I watched him swing his good leg down onto the floor again and attempt to stand up.

"I've got to find out," he said, as he slumped back down on the couch. "There's too much at stake."

"Andy, you don't know for sure that's where they are," Karen exclaimed.

"They're there," he insisted. "I know it."

"Just because John saw Steve," she said icily.

"Exactly because John spotted him. We'd never have guessed otherwise, would we? I can see what's happened," he went on. "They knew the package was coming up but weren't sure which of us would have it."

"And so?"

"They've been using the caravan at Bellsmore as a base. I'm sure of it."

"I knew something like this was going to happen, with all these new ideas at the Casino," Karen grumbled, as we watched Andy make a further attempt to get to his feet. Successful this time, he leaned over towards one of the wall units and swung the door open. Using it as a support, he hopped over and pulled a small box down off the shelf.

"I'm sorry you two had to get involved in this mess," he said to us, as he tugged at the lid. "It's the first time anything like this has ever gone wrong. From the inside, I mean."

"This'll only make matters worse, Andy," Karen pleaded, as we watched him caress the handle of a small, snub-nosed revolver he had taken out of the box.

What I was involved in now, made all my attempts to put things right in my life seem futile. These recent events – working at the Food Importers, the visits to my Great Aunt, selling fire extinguishers – seemed like mere fragments of a life that had now shattered into pieces. Even my relationship with Linda seemed to be ill-judged.

Now that I thought about it, how could it ever have seemed possible that someone like me could have formed the right kind of relationship with someone like her? Surely there was a huge inconsistency in this as much as there now seemed to be in everything else. Involved in her way of life, and in Andy's, I had never been able to fully identify with either of them.

But none of this mattered right now. As far as this business with the package was concerned I didn't need to fully identify with anybody. I knew enough about what I had got involved in to see that I was in very serious trouble. Not the kind of trouble I had ever been in before. And not something I could afford to sit and think about for very long, either.

"Give me the gun," I said, surprising even myself by my audacity, at which words Andy placed his hand over the weapon protectively.

"What's on your mind, John?" he asked, with raised eyebrows.

"One way or another I'm going to get the package back, Andy", I told him.

I listened as he said what I expected him to say. This wasn't a job for me. I was out of my depth. I had never used a gun in this way before while, with people like the smiling man in the lay-by, it would be second nature.

"Will I have to go without the gun?" I challenged.

Andy's words weren't going to make any difference, I knew, although they dispelled another point of uncertainty. "You could get killed," he told me.

"Don't be a fool, John," Karen chided. "This isn't your type of thing."

"How isn't it?" I asked. "What exactly is my type of thing? Do you really know?" I went on angrily, annoyed at being told by her that I wasn't equipped to deal with this kind of situation.

"Don't be a fool!" she repeated. "Andy, don't let him do this."

The truth was, I had to do it. How they saw it, wasn't the deciding factor. They were both saying what I knew myself anyway. I wasn't qualified for the job. But this was the very last straw. I had gone down in my own estimation just about as far as I was prepared to go.

Since leaving the Food Importers nothing had gone right for me. I hadn't asked anyone for help, except to forge a reference, and no one had offered any, except Andy. In all that time the only hand that had been lifted in my behalf had been his, and that fact had a life of its own. I knew that what I did now was going to say a lot about me.

And anyway, Karen seemed to be out of her depth in all this as much as I was, while Andy couldn't even walk. I had to do this, whether I was up to it or not.

"Do you actually know how to use this?" Andy asked scathingly, taking up the gun and laying it down flat in the palm of his outstretched hand.

"How will I know which caravan it is?" I asked him, ignoring his question. "Come on Andy, tell me."

"I'll show you," Karen said, taking us both by surprise.

"You're definitely not going, either of you," Andy said angrily. "Stop all this nonsense."

I watched him try to get to his feet again and, in the effort to do so, lay the gun back down on the table. As he stood on one leg trying to steady himself, I leaned over and picked up the weapon.

"I'm going and that's it," I said decisively, slipping the gun into my jacket pocket and stepping back towards the door.

Karen followed me out and, before I had time to think about it, she was sitting in the car beside me.

As we headed for the main road I wondered what my chances of getting the package back really were. I knew they weren't good. I was new to this kind of thing and these men would have the edge on me. They would be ruthless, I supposed, inclined to act without thinking while, with my track record, it would be the other way round.

But I had one thing in my favour. My role had changed. Like the smiling man taking me by surprise in the lay-by, I now had the hunter's advantage. It was possible that these men, probably Steve and the smiling man, would just be sitting there, like I had so recently been, unaware that they were in any immediate danger.

chapter
two

As we drove along the dual carriageway I wished I could put the clock back to where I had been just a few weeks ago, sitting in the sales office with Benny, instead of here behind the wheel of a car that could be taking me on a one-way journey.

The first to arrive that morning, I had been re-reading the polite but threatening letter about my mortgage arrears. And something else had been bothering me, too. Although I had been in sales for years, it was beginning to dawn on me that I wasn't really a salesman at heart. I had never come close to being a good liar, like so many salesman these days, or a good number of lawyers and politicians too for that matter. But here in Bartons I was certainly heading in what I thought was the right, or was it the wrong direction.

It had been nothing at all like this in my previous job, at the Food Importers. The work there had been entirely different, with nothing even remotely like the 'hard sell' about it. I had quite enjoyed it, with its reasonable salary and generous car allowance. My position there as a sales administrator had suited me. I had been good at analysing my problems and sticking to clearly defined objectives in my efforts to solve them, although it was something I had picked up from one of the books I had found in the attic that had put me ahead of most of my colleagues. It was a work that contained details from the Congressional Report on the causes of the great naval disaster at Pearl Harbour in 1941 where the Japanese planes had caught the Americans by surprise. No mention here of a global plot by Roosevelt, I had noticed at once. Officers at the Base and their seniors in Washington, the Report had solemnly declared, had largely been to blame, although Kimmel and Short, the head naval and military men seem to have been victims rather than perpetrators of the inefficient procedures prevalent there at that time. But generally speaking commanders at the base and the hierarchy in Washington were said to be in the habit of giving important orders the effectiveness of which they had seldom taken the time or felt they had had the opportunity to verify. No one seemed to realise, the Report had gone on to state accusingly, that the duties of an administrator were only half-completed upon the issuance of an order. It was equally important, and an integral part of the job, to ensure that an order was properly understood and carried out, which was manifestly not being done to the extent that it should have been. A lot of the planes and ships had been lost because of neglect of such principles and I saw to it in my job as an administrator that I didn't make the same mistake.

I also made as much use as I could of several of the other twenty-four odd points the Report had made, rightly considering them to be gems of wisdom that even today, perhaps even more so today than ever, could, if heeded, turn many a struggling business enterprise or other such organisation in to something that was highly efficient and successful, which could go a long way towards putting the country back on its feet. But people as a whole just didn't get it, I had found.

'What a fanciful and extravagant claim I had just made' I knew would be the judgement passed on me by my peers and by my superiors. And so I kept my thoughts to myself, but unlike these American officers I let nothing slip through the net and monitored every loose end as an administrator with a vengeance.

To avoid falling out with my peers, who adhered to the more orthodox and reactive, 'pass the buck' approach, I used my knowledge of these 'pearls' of wisdom like a secret weapon, appearing to be merely conscientious and hard-working.

My face had fitted, too. I don't suppose I would have got a job in this thriving, long-established business if it hadn't. Like the candidates for officer selection I had read about in another of these books I had found in the attic, I had had to score very high at the initial interview, by appearing to be the right type. Without this, as it was with certain would-be officers, only a genius among them would subsequently have been able to scrape up enough points to qualify. In my particular case, having gone to a 'right' school seemed to have got me 'off the hook' and into the job.

Safe in this zone of security, I had been able to keep my distance from the world outside and, with a faintly superior attitude, observe the Scottish scene, or was it mainly just the Glasgow scene, a city where speculation about what might be worn, or not be worn, under an important part of the national dress was not considered racially offensive and where the shortage of people actually wearing the kilt didn't mean there was no national pride. But the fact that policemen were seen even less than kilted citizens, except on television or at big football matches, I felt was another matter. Didn't this allow perverts and psychopaths who had been turned loose after serving their latest sentences, and who were already prowling about like wild animals, to seek out their pray with a little more freedom than they deserved.

But in other ways the city was quite safe, populated as it was by Roman Catholics and Protestants who were all friends and who were hardly, if ever, at each other's throats, in spite of the fact that many of them still went to different churches and to different schools. These indigenous citizens almost all thought there were far too many immigrants while the main political parties, their fingers on their own pulse rather than the nation's, advised that more were needed, pointing out that we were all immigrants just a few hundred years ago and reminding us of what we did or didn't do in India and places like that.

If there were other serious anomalies in the way things were being run in this major city of a country that was determined to bring democracy to other less fortunate peoples, the two which made the most impression on me were the frail hospital patients in flimsy dressing gowns and on wheelchairs who were forced to smoke outside in the cold. Who were the people who voted for that? I wondered., and would they have administered such strong medicine in the days of Roosevelt, Churchill and Stalin, especially to the latter, as the Big Three smoked their way to victory over their great non-smoking adversary? And what about the planning applications which were objected to by hundreds of locals and approved by one stranger? What was so democratic about his vote? And what did the word 'consultations' which he had held with the existing resident voters actually mean, when he never seemed to listen to anyone.

Fortunately the number of people taking further education, which at least dispensed knowledge if not wisdom, had greatly increased, as had the number of TV channels now available, although the results, in both cases, seemed to be quantitative rather than qualitative. And it was good, too, that the moral standards expected of people in certain occupations were still supposed to be high, except for the fact that, although more of these people were being found wanting, fewer of them were being sacked, none of them were resigning and almost all of them were scrambling after knighthoods, and taking home big pensions.

I also thought it strange that people who would object to strangers walking into their house, or even into their garden, people who would jealously guard any advantages they might have gained in life from the sacrifices made by their parents or grandparents, seemed unable to prevent a huge number of foreigners from wandering quite freely into their country. That many of their immediate forebears had been blown to smithereens on the ground, in the air and on the sea in their efforts to save the country from 'invasion' surely meant that something was wrong. Were people suffering from a kind of national amnesia or from an abysmal ignorance of recent history? Or was it just that they were too indifferent to get angry at those responsible for leaving the borders open and, for their unwillingness to admit to or to undo the damage that they were so obviously doing in leaving the front door key on top of the mat instead of under it?

But with money in the bank and living in a nice house in a nice district, with a nice car and job security, none of this had seemed too important. Compared to some places, Glasgow was still a good place to live in. It never occurred to me that without my comfortable standard of living and reasonably secure background, I might have taken a more jaundiced view.

'What in God's name is happening to our country?' I might have asked myself.

I didn't get as far as this intellectually, however, and any serious emotional involvement I had at that time centred mainly on my dealings with the opposite sex. In this, there had been quite a few exciting disappointments offset by a sufficient number of successes to keep me going and give me something to aim for in life.

I could also look back on a happy boyhood, living in that nice house in that nice district with my late mother's very much older sister, Grace. I had been too young to be scarred either by my father's early death in an accident overseas or by my mother's death from natural causes not long afterwards.

Aunt Grace, more like a grandmother than a mother, had exercised a strong influence for the good on me without exerting too much pressure and I took for granted the good education she had given me and the good job it had helped me to get.

So far in my adult life, I had experienced only one serious crisis when Grace, much against her will, had had to go into residential care. The fact that she only had life-rent on our house, which had expired when she gave up her occupancy, rendered me homeless. I also learned soon afterwards, that she had much less in the bank than everyone thought. If she was to remain secure in the Home of her choice there was a shortfall that only I could make up.

Nothing was more important to me than Aunt Grace's welfare and before long I had signed a few forms and made out a Direct Debit for the required amount. Having a good job, I at the same time obtained a mortgage on a small, well-appointed flat and, as is often the case in circumstances like these, the amount of money didn't seem too important. I was more anxious about having to make all my own meals and iron my own shirts. Although I missed my Aunt Grace a lot, I managed to weather the storm and was soon able to get back to my golf, my music, my books and, of course, my pursuit of the opposite sex.

Being quite good at my job, quite popular, quite good-looking and quite good with women, were qualities I felt quite pleased about. They were things I didn't have to worry about too much, I would tell myself, occasionally, when it occurred to me that I lacked ambition. 'Quite' seemed to be my personal adverb. It was quite good standing still, and quite good feeling that I had things under control.

Although I was relatively unambitious in my job, I was next in line to be Deputy Manager and felt quite strongly that I deserved to move up a rung. Instead, something happened that set in motion a chain of events which would destroy my complacency and bring my sheltered existence to an end. My kindly, efficient and highly-appreciative boss announced his retiral!

At that time I hadn't realised how lucky I was to be working for a man like him. For many people, describing the boss's shortcomings could take up a lot of time in the pub, and thinking about him, at other times, too, could keep them off their sleep. It wasn't that way with me. I was like the young German Officer I had read about in yet another of these books I had found, who had laid out the maps wrongly at Hitler's Situation Conference, causing the famous Field Marshal Guderian to stop in mid-sentence and glare at him, causing Hitler, of all people, to sink back in his chair in an even worse state, and the assembled generals to stare at him aghast. My boss had been more like Grand Admiral Doenitz who had smiled at the young officer, offered a few consoling words, and lifted the pile of maps up for him to put in the right order, the kind of human touch not too evident these days in certain quarters, I felt.

But my luck in having a boss like this had run out. I was about to discover that this old man, who could run a business and actually be a nice person at the same time, had a son who didn't take after him. To my dismay the heir at once showed himself adept in the mis-use of power and the promotion I felt I deserved went to someone whose face he seemed to prefer to mine and who, everybody with any sense knew, couldn't do the job.

As far as the Food Importers went it was all downhill after that, and a set of circumstances connected to the Annual Staff Dance brought matters to a head.

In the first place, the new boss's partner wasn't someone I should have asked to dance, but free drinks, on top of pent-up emotion, caused me to ignore the 'keep off the grass' sign and go on to make an even more serious error of judgement. The effect of this was compounded by the fact that she had drunk as much as I had.

I learned afterwards that she had had a base motive in allowing me to steer her into the bar. The new boss had been paying too much attention to one of his secretaries and, in retaliation, his partner had decided to pay too much attention to me. Things went from bad to worse and, from the bar, down a dark corridor into an ante room, where the air at once became filled with the smell of mixed drinks exhaled by our heavy breathing. As we indulged in the athletic posturing and exchange of warm kisses sanctioned by my slamming of the door I realised that the absence of a lock and key made what I intended to be my next move very risky. The act of complete abandon that this would signify surely required a degree of privacy greater than that afforded by a room with an unlocked door. But that wasn't what stopped me. Nor was it the fact that I had a strong strain of the gentleman in me. It had just occurred to me that the new boss might have something to say about where I was and what I was doing and I suspected, even then, that I had made a very serious mistake. I had. Our journey to the ante room had not gone unreported, and the new boss's opinion of me as a sales administrator changed accordingly. The deadly threat that this posed to my peace of mind made it hard for me to disguise my feelings and the new boss, annoyed that I seemed to think as little of him as he did of me, persevered in his attempts to blame me for things that weren't my fault. And so, one day, when he kept telling me that his mistake was mine, and the tension had become unbearable, I did something that was easy and which made me feel good at the time. I walked out.

*

Unemployed for the first time in my life I hated the ambivalence in my friends' response to my plight. While they said they sympathised with me, even admired me for my brave act, they themselves seemed determined to stay on good terms with my 'persecutor'. Had they been lying to me when they said they detested him even more than I did? Disgusted by their 'two-faced' behaviour, I decided to withdraw to the flat and keep my own company for a while.

At that point it was pride, rather than earnings that seemed to be the issue. Brought up not having to give too much thought to money, certainly not with regard to where my next meal or the one after that was coming from, I had never learned to respect its power. And anyway I was sure for a while that a suitable new employer existed somewhere, anywhere.

Aware that I didn't have a reference, I quickly set about writing one of my own to have it copied onto firm's notepaper and signed by a friend. Not doing too well, I decided instead to make use of a 'reference' which had caught my attention whilst thumbing through one of these books – 'I was absolutely trustworthy, upright and direct. My mental and bodily hygiene was excellent. My appearance indicated no wrong inclinations, no addictions. My intellectual and physical predispositions were excellent.'

As I read it back I, of course, began to have second thoughts. Although it gave quite an accurate picture of me it was a bit too glowing, and it seemed sort of old-fashioned, too. It was only when I decided to look more closely at the book I had taken it from that I found out on the next page what the person, being described in the 'reference' by his commanding officer, had done in his job as a camp physician at Auschwitz Extermination Camp. He had for example conducted gruesome experiments on any prisoner – man, woman or child – within his reach and had, as a matter of course, increased the number of hospital beds available by having the existing patients murdered. In the face of such barbarity I quickly decided to discard the infamous Nazi doctor, Josef Mengele's reference and write another one which would make a good person seem better rather than an evil person sound good.

But if the employer I had in mind did indeed exist the fact that I couldn't find him soon changed the nature of my problem. The amount in my deposit account kept for a rainy day disappeared after a few rainy months leaving me with arrears in my mortgage repayments and a headache in meeting most of my other commitments, too.

Unfortunately I found that letting my credit cards take the strain only increased it, and when I at last took stock, I discovered I owed about the equivalent of half a year's salary to my various creditors, which seemed about right, since I had been living off their money for the best part of six months.

With mounting debts, and a growing anxiety about what might happen to my Aunt Grace in the Home if I fell into arrears there, too, I had no alternative but to review my approach to the job market. Working in the Sales Department of a Fire Protection Company would normally have been the furthest thing from my mind but, feeling not a little unnerved by my money worries, the occupation took on a new appeal. Surely helping people to put our fires was a good cause?

chapter
three

IN MY NEW JOB AT BARTON FIRE PROTECTION, IT
wasn't long before I had familiarised myself with the four main
types of fire extinguisher, only stumbling over the existence,
and the name, of a fifth type, the recently discontinued BCF,
whose full name, Bromochloridefluoromethane, must speak
for itself, since no-one can pronounce it.

Once considered the most versatile extinguisher on the
market, capable of putting anything out, including the dog,
the significance of this extinguisher now lay in the fact that it
had to be replaced, because of the harmful effect its emissions
were having on the ozone layer. That fire extinguisher salesman
could unashamedly try to sell replacement extinguishers for
the very ones that they had only fairly recently spoken so
highly of, said something about their occupation.

As did the fact that it was standard practice among
these salesmen to strike terror into the hearts of their sales
prospects by painting a vivid picture of the perils faced by

anyone not buying their product. They might be shut down by the Fire Department, or burned to death. These unfortunate beneficiaries also had to be persuaded that the discount they were being offered on the replacement extinguishers, was in effect a charitable gift that would ensure their survival.

It didn't take me long to find out that in Bartons, profit-making rather than fire extinguishing, was the driving force, which was fair enough in today's world, except for the fact that in my job I was expected to make it seem, to an absolutely ridiculous extent, that it was the other way round. Since this kind of subterfuge meant subordinating all the technical facts and figures to the demands of the hidden agenda I began to have anxious thoughts about the true nature of the work that lay ahead of me.

I was starting out all over again, at the bottom of the ladder. Not the fireman's ladder, since you weren't allowed to go up that one – portable extinguishers were only suitable for dealing with small fires.

The right ladder, however, had its limitations, too. I was beginning to fear that the ability to climb up it, hadn't been embedded in my genes. All I seemed to have inherited was a sense of belonging to a class of people who hadn't had to worry too much about money, and whose reasonable position on the social scale was their divine right rather than the result of past economic success. I could see that the contents of the letter from the Building Society were threatening not just my financial standing but my sense of identity.

It wasn't that the sum asked for was all that much, amounting as it did to little more than what I might have earned in six months. But this would be a long time, particularly in Barton Fire, I could see, when evaluated in terms of taking all the abuse I was getting from the owner, Sears, and telling all those half-truths to potential customers.

Since I couldn't save all my salary anyway, such a comparison only served to emphasise the hopelessness of the situation and I could see that my attainment level in this matter was approaching that of a financial imbecile. My comfortable, self-appointed place in life as a kind of self-educated intellectual, qualified for this by my disposition rather than by my state, was becoming untenable.

*

Although the sales office at Barton's wasn't actually dingy, like most of the people who worked in dingy offices I could find plenty of other reasons for not wanting to be there. It had one redeeming feature, however. There were some colourful pictures on the walls, one of which had been a great help to me.

It was a quiet country scene – a bridge, a shallow river with ducks on it, and some people from the eighteenth century, or thereabouts, strolling along the riverbank. I had often escaped into this silent world and walked along beside these people.

"Has Sears come in yet?" I asked Benny, as he settled at his desk.

"He has indeed," Benny drawled. "Walked past me in the corridor as usual as if I didn't exist."

This was typical of Sears, I thought, as I evaluated Benny's comment. My tormentor and boss always had a way of advertising his presence. Even when you, yourself, didn't pass him in the corridor, some other invisible person usually did.

I noticed that Benny, just like our boss, seemed unconcerned about his image. What was he like? I asked myself, as I looked sluggishly over at him, with his mop of thick, black hair, always kept saturated in hair cream and neatly combed in place. He had to be colour blind – with his pink shirt, grey tie and blue suit. But there was something about Benny I liked. As a colleague I felt he was someone you could trust. He wouldn't often try to take the credit for other people's hard work, and if he was moody from time to time he would never act unpleasantly or unhelpfully towards you because of it. In fact I don't think he had a spiteful bone in his body and I didn't think it was his fault that he wasn't very good at his job.

But there was also something about him I didn't like, although I could understand it. He was always trying to please Sears, and would adopt an almost worshipful demeanour when talking to him. He reminded me of something one of the wives of Kim Philby, a senior British diplomat in one of these books, who had spied with outstanding success for Stalin, once said about her husband. Mrs Philby had observed in this particular book from the attic, that her husband had always been pathetically hungry for the approbation of his Russian masters, 'Throw him a few crumbs of praise and his spirits would respond like the tail of Pavlov's dog'. This was just like Benny, I observed, although there were fewer occasions like this in his life, with Sears rather than Stalin as his Master, than there were in Philby's.

Benny was married with two children, two lovely children, recent photographs of whom he displayed on his desk and any even more recent photographs of whom he never tired of showing you. The fact that he was Jewish said more to me than the photographs did however, for he certainly belied the description given of Jews in another passage from one of these books where, in a summing up of what certain Europeans were said to have thought of them prior to the Second World War – Jews were avaricious liars, untrustworthy, opportunistic and money-worshipping. Could anyone really be as bad as this? I had thought at the time?

This definitely wasn't Benny, I could plainly see. It seemed more like a description of Sears and it could also be any one of a number of Scotsmen I was descended from. But then weren't the Scots, coming as some of them did from Scythia, once thought to be a lost tribe of Israel, and this by educated people who had actually written books on the subject. Maybe that explained it. But poor Benny!

Apart from this vague connection and our mutual need to sell fire extinguishers for Sears, I felt I didn't have much in common with Benny but having the threat of repossession hanging over my head, of actually being put out of my house, had given rise to feelings that I supposed were not unlike what Benny's fellow Jews in Europe had experienced when they were being hounded by the Nazis. Being thrown out on the street as they were, and as I might be too, if things didn't look up, was only faintly suggestive of what had ultimately happened to them, and yet the very idea of eviction alone was almost more than I could take.

But regardless of all this I thought it a good thing that I bore Benny no ill will for hadn't the Pastor pointed out that the Jews were still beloved of God and it simply wasn't true, as some equally religious people kept saying, that they were totally disowned and rejected. In fact the principle 'Anti-Semitism will be punished' was very much in force and always had been, since the time of Abraham, the Pastor was often at pains to point out, too. I therefore relished the idea that Sears, in his treatment of Benny and of course myself, wasn't, according to the application of this principle, going to escape unpunished.

But the Pastor went even further than this, as he did with a lot of things. According to him the whole Church, including his own, was like the branch of an olive tree, a wild branch at that, which had been grafted on to another olive tree, a cultivated one, whose natural branches were the Jews. So that, as far as my attitude to Benny was concerned, this meant that Benny was all right, a Jewish Scot and not a Scottish Jew. I still wasn't sure what I was myself, as if it mattered, Celtic-Norse, Norse-Celtic or just a plain Viking, and that was only on my mother's side.

I needed the picture on the wall this morning, to take my mind off the mess I was in. I felt like a prisoner more than ever, and knew I had to serve out my sentence in this place if I was to keep my creditors at bay. Joining the people in the picture, walking along at a respectable distance behind them, I began to feel better.

But not for long. My salary was only half what it had been at the Food Importers. So far, it had been earned sitting at my desk processing incoming telephone enquiries about servicing fire extinguishers and I craved the additional amount Sears had assured me I would be able to make on commission from sales. But it wasn't easy to close a sale on the telephone and the lead often had to be passed to an outside sales rep. The ten percent commission Sears had promised became only 5% when I had to share it with the other person.

Even if I could, on occasion, close a sale on the telephone, to someone who had perhaps read our ad in the Trade Directory, I had no control over the frequency with which this might occur. So results depended more on luck than on skill and as long as I remained a mere appendage to the telephone they weren't going to get any better.

And even if he did send me out 'on the road', I had no idea how I would get on. It seemed that my sales and my overall circumstances were being sucked into the same black hole.

I looked up at the picture again, my eyes coming to rest on the houses in the background. I wished I could take up residence in a room behind one of the little windows that faced out onto the river. I imagined the people strolling on the path were my neighbours and I peered at them intently, making out the familiar features of the pleasant-looking, elderly man and his young female companion. The girl looked like she was the man's daughter, but I often imagined her to be Linda. The thought of Linda was pleasant, but unsettling, as it usually was.

Picking up the pile of sales leads from the tray and skimming through them I could see that most of them were worthless. They were really just the names and addresses of some of the bigger firms who had been customers in the past and might therefore, according to Sears' ridiculous optimism, be expected to buy again. But they would buy again when it suited them, I knew, not when somebody like me phoned up from Bartons to put the idea into their heads. Phoning them up was about as likely to produce a sale as was waiting on them to phone you. Sears had set a target for calls like this and the usual anguish and torment was present in the process.

From my in-depth experience at the Food Importers, I could see that Sears was a fairly typical second generation owner, devoid of the true understanding that only experience brings and filled with enthusiasm for his stupid ideas. He didn't have what it takes, personally, to make many good sales in a competitive market place. Other people had to do it for him. That they were experienced and knew more about the intricacies of the work then he did, never seemed to bother him.

The way he coped with this inadequacy, on a day to day basis, was quite simple. A drop in the figures, a failure to close a sale, were always caused by his staff, who didn't work hard enough, or weren't good enough at their job.

I noticed that Benny was looking at the sales leads tray too.

"They don't look up to much," he muttered as he lifted the phone.

When he had finished and the accuracy of his assessment had been confirmed, I diverted my eyes from the emptiness of the Sales Made tray and stared at the refreshment table.

"Me too," said Benny.

I felt that things couldn't get much worse at that point. But I was wrong. The door opened and I turned to see Sears, the very man himself, standing in the doorway and looking very much in our direction.

chapter
four

Tall and thin with fair hair, watery eyes and large, uneven teeth, Sears wasn't a man of flesh and blood. Having a huge pool of labour to draw on, he played with his employees, like a child with toy soldiers, disposing of them and replacing them at will, so I had been told, without any valid reason, and attributing the huge turnover in staff to anything other than his own involvement in it.

That something should be done about people like him was a thought that occurred to me daily. Like the new boss I had left behind at the Food Importers, Sears had only got where he was by an accident of birth, which had even helped him to win a seat on the local Council representing the very people he despised. He was a leader without leadership qualities, I felt, who didn't know how to manage his employees without oppressing them. He seemed to assume that his superior position actually made him superior while what he really was he obviously managed to hide, from himself I felt, and from many people who should have known better.

"Morning," came his abrupt greeting. "Early with the coffee, aren't you?"

'Was I supposed to agree with this?', I asked myself, aware that I was becoming allergic to this man, who always spoke in a tone of voice that suggested he disapproved of you, who always knew best, who never owned up to being wrong.

"How are the leads going?" he asked us.

"We're getting through them, Mr Sears." Benny told him weakly.

"That's not what I asked you. Have you made any actual sales?" Sears blurted out in reply.

"No, but ..."

"And you Grant?"

"No. We didn't expect to ..." I began to explain.

"You don't put enough effort into it" he snapped, cutting me off.

Here it was, hard work, only hard work and, of course, your hard work, was the answer to everything.

"It's the leads," I felt I had to say. "They're all for existing customers, Mr Sears."

His watery eyes bulged and "What's wrong with that?" he sneered. "It's existing customers who have got us where we are."

"But they don't buy until they really need something," I countered, almost in a whisper.

"Well that's what I'm paying you for. Talk them into it."

It was no use. The man just couldn't grasp the fact that hard work and wasted effort could sometimes be the same thing.

"It's time you got out of the office and canvassed some shops," he said to me. There's a lot of people out there. Why are so many of them taking their business elsewhere?"

The situation was absolutely hopeless, I felt, as the door closed behind him. His ability to misdirect and discourage your efforts was proving to be much better than my judgement had been, in coming to work here. But at least he was sending me 'out on the road', although 'how many shopkeepers actually needed a fire extinguisher, anyway?' I asked myself. If a bucket of water wouldn't do it, surely the best and cheapest course of action for most of them would be to make for the door.

There had to be a better way of going about things than this, I felt. Why did all the ideas have to his while all the blame would be mine?

With my kind of personality, it wasn't enough just to do what people usually did when they were in a situation like this. It wasn't enough just to hate him in silence, or mutter that he was born out of wedlock. Instead, I felt compelled to identify and dissect the kind of evil he perpetrated, to put it into a broader perspective than the world of fire extinguishers and sales targets. And I was greatly helped to do this by making constant reference to my collection of books.

On first discovering these in the attic, carefully packed into two huge boxes, I had at first just browsed through them, only gradually becoming aware of their true worth. As a Scotsman, on both sides of the family, it had been an eye-opener to find out in one of the first books I looked at that a lot of us had originated in Greater Scythia and had crossed the Tyrrhenian Sea to get here. It was even more interesting to learn too that Adolf Hitler had thought very highly of us as soldiers, and had said so in Mein Kampf, unlike another great butcher, the Duke of Cumberland, who had tried to destroy any evidence that was left of this by ordering the shooting to kill of the fleeing and bedraggled remnants of Charles' army at Culloden in 1745.

But to me these books were much more than just a way of gaining a knowledge or understanding of significant events. They weren't just history books. I had found some of them contained things which I would often see, in essence, being re-enacted around me.

For the most part the books, in the box easiest to get at, were concerned with personalities and events in recent history and had a lot to say about both World Wars. But there were some on religion, and one or two on gardening, too.

I didn't bother with the last of these, and I seldom opened the ones on religion, at least not until I encountered Pastor Mackenzie, that is.

Inclined to be a deep thinker, or at least accused of being one by Aunt Grace, amongst others, perhaps in surprise because of my ability to fail exams, it definitely seemed to me that many of the events described in these books bore a strong resemblance not only to what was going on in the world around me but also to what was actually going on in my own life.

Although there didn't seem to be anything wrong in identifying with the characters and events in these books the practice was sufficiently unusual to make me wonder, on occasion, just what lay behind it. For instance could I be like the Jewish American film star who confessed to reading avidly on the Holocaust because the sufferings described there had made him feel better able to face up to his own more everyday and less severe sufferings?

Or was I just escaping from reality, like the Allied Supreme Commander General Eisenhower was when reading between, and even during battles, cowboy books and possibly seeing the odd encounter shaping up like the gunfight at the OK Coral? But what was the harm in it? Neither of us thought for one minute that we had actually become the protagonist and would need a change of clothes.

And there was also the fact that military history and drama were closely connected. Surely I was just putting some added meaning into life and gaining valuable insights into the human condition along the way.

And wasn't this a good thing when 1066, 1314 and a king with six wives were all I could remember from school, and not much less than I had remembered at exam time. Surely as an adult it was now important to get these things into perspective. For example, the average number of wives got through by one man was quite high these days but Henry VIII's achievement, although perhaps not his methods, were something that should be kept in mind.

People like Sears were everywhere, I read in one of the books, in all classes and in all countries and it wasn't always power that made them corrupt, as was commonly thought. Many of them were corrupt from the start. Power was only a vehicle not a first cause. While Sears didn't indulge in the overt acts of violence of the SS guard described in one particular book, he nevertheless had the same malicious disposition. He knew he had you in his power. You were a kind of prisoner who couldn't easily escape from him because of the mortgage repayments you had to make, amongst other things, and the slim chance you had of finding another job.

He could threaten, bully and insult you, just like the guards did in a Nazi concentration camp. In any attempt to explain the horrors of the camps, and indeed the many similar barbarities that occurred outside them the plentiful existence of people like Sears, often in the most unlikely of places, couldn't be left out.

He was forever cutting the rate of commission. What could a prisoner have said to having his rations reduced in this way? What could I say to him?

He didn't physically abuse and kill, as did the SS guard, but the difference in behaviour was one of degree, not of kind. I felt sure that if he had looked for work in the SS, and been given an aptitude test, he would have been a very successful candidate.

To put it simply, I was working for a heartless employer, had the status of a camp inmate, and the feeling that I had not dissimilar prospects. God forgive me for my overstatement, although it should be kept in mind that a bad toothache is still very bad, even if it won't kill you.

But what had I got myself into?

Andy came into the office to save me from my thoughts, I felt, as he smiled over at me.

A few inches above average height, he had dark brown hair, slightly thinning at the front, and a strong, intelligent look about him. Although more than a pound or two beyond having an athletic build, he seemed to be in peak condition. He didn't look like he belonged in this place. His suit hung well on him and he had a military bearing, except for a certain casualness in his manner. Wearing a pleasant, faintly amused expression when talking to you, his features would often take on what seemed to be an intense, supportive look, as if, while not yet having fully appraised what you had just said, he nevertheless sympathised with you and was on your side. I often wondered how he had ended up in a place like this. Although I knew he wouldn't move in the same circles as me, not that I had any circles now, except under my eyes, he was one of the few people in Bartons I could seriously tolerate.

"Where to tonight, John?" he asked me.

"Nowhere special."

"Do you fancy a drink?"

"I certainly do."

"I'm buying tonight. How about the Old Toll Bar, in Cartvale Road. I'll introduce you to Karen, and of course Big Tom, and some of the others. I've been meaning to ask you for some time."

When he had gone, I sat for a while listening to Benny at work on the telephone. At first, because of the poor quality of the leads, I had to admire his enthusiasm, but since Clausewitz, the great Prussian strategist, had said in one of the books in the Collection, that determination proceeds from a strong mind rather than a brilliant one, and Benny had neither, it didn't surprise me when he soon began to falter, looking frustrated and discouraged. Wellington, too, on the next page of the same book, had cursed his cavalry for being like this – unduly high-spirited at the start of a venture and unduly low spirited when it didn't instantly succeed. And he should have known since he routed Napoleon for us at Waterloo in 1815.

Benny's strong point was really the computer, I knew, although he was inclined to spoil it by not updating the Sales Sheets often enough. The computer, like the famous fictional gunfighter, Shane, had once said about his particular weapon of choice, was only as good or as bad as the man who used it. In this respect I felt Sears deserved Benny whose shortcomings helped him to be as ill-informed as he often was.

*

Before I even looked up at the picture on the Sales Office wall, I knew the girl in it was going to be Linda again. It was warm and sunny on the depicted riverbank, just as it was outside in the real world, too. I longed to get out of the place and drive up to see her.

I knew that this wouldn't be as undemanding as an imaginary stroll along the riverbank for, in the real world, there had been nothing between Linda and me but smiles and polite words. To think of her in the way I had been doing, and to give her such a prominent place in the picture, was something fifteen year old boys would be inclined to do. I didn't have anything tangible to build my hopes on.

Meeting someone like her in the way that I did had taken me completely by surprise. I had only gone to the church to please Aunt Grace. For years I had successfully resisted her efforts to get me to attend regularly and dropping her off at the door in bad weather was usually as near as I got.

I would do anything for my Aunt Grace, anything I could, but from the occasional visits to church I had made over the years I had formed a picture in my mind's eye of what it involved and had decided it definitely wasn't for me. It was only when she was leaving to take up residence in the Home and brought up the subject of my 'heathenship', like a valedictory address, that I felt constrained to give in. I could go, maybe once or twice, even introduce myself to the new minister she thought so highly of. It didn't seem too much to ask. The idea of Aunt Grace no longer being around to look after me had affected my judgement more than I realised at the time.

On my first visit I decided to sit near the back and, having arrived a few minutes early, I brooded on the preponderance of bald heads and grey hair in the view from the rear that was confronting me. There was a smattering of younger female heads and shoulders, too, which looked more interesting. But this was hardly the place for that. Generally speaking I felt bored, but not too out of place, even if I was.

When Linda came in and sat in the row in front slightly to my left, everything changed. I felt almost dazzled by the beautiful sheen on her hair, and I could see just enough of her profile to make it difficult for me to take my eyes off her. The way I had to squint at her to avoid attracting attention, made me feel undignified. But I was anything but bored now. What did she look like from the front? I kept asking myself.

The new minister, I soon discovered, wasn't someone you were likely to forget, either, once you had heard what he had to say. For the next few weeks, he announced, his sermons were going to touch on a subject that could effect most of the people on the planet.

Climate Change as a sermon was far from what I had expected so when he described some of its manifestations and placed these in a Biblical context I was surprised enough to listen.

Beginning at the beginning, as he put it, which was the book of Genesis, he read out in a firm clear voice from Genesis 19, verses 18 and 19 – 'And the sons of Noah that went forth from the ark were Shem, Ham and Japheth and of them was the whole earth overspread.'

His voice and demeanour made it plain that to him this was an historical fact not a geological controversy over how much of the earth had actually been covered by the alleged flood.

Twelve families came from Japheth, he continued, twenty-six from Ham and twenty from Shem, each family being given its own language and its own land and thereafter becoming a nation.

'And so we have the origin of the fifty-eight basic nations,' he had declared.

Going on to describe the Japhetic group of families as belonging to the northern parts of the earth, the families of Ham to the southern parts, and the Semitic group to the central belt, the new minister drew attention to how those living in lush river valleys would have a different physique and character from those living on hilly, infertile regions and that the people of one nation would be very different from those of another.

When he went on to talk about the development of Israel from Abraham or Abram, as he was then called, and some later additions and developments, I felt he had at least excluded himself from the contemporary world view. Racial distinctions and national borders, according to his way of looking at things, proceeded from God. That there should be one nation of men wasn't in line with the natural order of things, according to him, and in keeping with this, only one hundred years after the Flood, the Tower of Babel, the symbol of human unity, had been summarily destroyed.

So much for the multi-cultural society I had thought at this point, seeing a connection between what the Pastor was saying and what someone in the Book Collection had said on a not dissimilar subject. Schact, the great German banker of the period between the two World Wars, found to be not guilty of war crimes, had reminded his countrymen that culture and civilisation weren't the same thing and that it was dangerous to ignore the difference. Culture had its roots in religion and any country which relegated it to mere reason and enlightenment would lose its soul. Civilisation, for its part, didn't have a soul.

The Pastor's world view, far as it was from mainstream thinking, didn't seem so outlandish at this stage. Schact had gone on to point out in words that could indeed have been the Pastor's own, that the religion of his country (Germany) was Christian and that its cultural direction should never be handed over to people of other religions although, of course, it was of paramount importance that such people should be treated with the same affection, respect and support as everyone else.

That Germany had trampled the latter part of Schact's advice under foot with such disastrous and infernal consequences surely gave some strength to what the Pastor was saying. He was surely at least worth listening to.

As Linda stood up at the end of the service and turned to leave, my thoughts on who or who not to listen to instantly lost their appeal. She was dressed formally in a dark costume and looked striking, with a smooth complexion, beautiful brown eyes, and well-shaped lips. Her long dark hair and interesting profile had been sending out the right signals.

But how could I hope that the visits I had afterwards made to the café with her meant she thought about me in the same way I thought about her? Our conversations had usually been about the sermon and, since the café was on the way home, our visits there hadn't been actual dates, only dates to me in my mind's eye.

That Linda liked me was not in doubt. She was always nice and polite to me and quick enough at catching my eye in the church grounds after the service. Her willingness to walk with me on the way home was surely a very positive feature, if nothing more than that, I told myself.

Unfortunately, the relationship hadn't developed much further than this. In the café, I had mostly agreed with her in conversations about her beliefs and since, as I had soon learned, she was the Minister's daughter, I had kept most of my troublesome opinions to myself. We had got on very well, indeed, therefore, by certain standards. But had there really been anything else between us? This was something I was going to have to find out. I had to. Looking back on it, I could see now that I had used the fact that I had walked out of my job as an excuse and had, in a sense, walked out on Linda and the church too. In deciding to keep my own company for a while, I had thought I could leave the interest I had in her until later. I had felt I needed a rest from the strong impression the Pastor was making on me, and had quite wrongly thought that I had needed a rest from Linda too. It was time to put the matter right.

chapter
five

As I reached the outskirts of the town I realised I could hardly say to Linda that I was just passing through the district by chance. If I was, where was I headed? Nobody passed through the outlying village in which she stayed except tradesmen and neighbouring residents.

My timing wasn't good either except for the fact that I remembered a mid-week social event was sometimes held about then in the Church Hall.

I envied those rich emigrants, I had often read about, returning home after they had made their fortune overseas. Instead, here I was, returning too in a sense, but worse off than I had ever been before.

The church hall was well lit up and I could see, beyond a crowd gathered at the entrance, that a dance was in progress. But what now? 'So much for being proactive', I lamented under my breath.

From the doorway I was able to take in most of the dance

floor. If she was here, she wasn't dancing. I inched my way down the side and took in the four corners of the hall, my eyes scanning the faces of the women gathered at the refreshment table, too.

At last I spotted her. She was sitting with someone at the side of the hall, watching the dancers. I could see that her companion was a refined, pleasant looking man of about my own age. From where she sat, mine would be only one in a sea of faces on the other side of the dance floor, which allowed me to peer over at her, like a plain-clothes policeman on surveillance, while I decided what to do.

Melting into the crowd at the refreshment table, I hoped, I poured myself a cup of tea and tried to gather my thoughts. The direct approach, I felt strongly, now that I was beginning to get my bearings, wouldn't do. Telling her I had come all this way just to see her didn't sound right, especially not if it was in the presence of an unknown male companion. I leaned over the table and stared blankly at the food.

Anxiously turning to continue my surveillance, I was in time to see that she and her companion had risen to their feet, about to join the dancers. Fearful she might spot me on her way round the floor and still having no idea what I was going to say to her, I decided to think rather than act.

Getting back in the car, I sat for a while scanning the dashboard for inspiration. It would be better to start again tomorrow, I finally concluded. And anyway, a dance hall was not really a good place for a meeting of this kind. I went over it all again. Would she be really pleased to see me, or had I misjudged the relationship to the extent that her response would be one of near-indifference?

No further on in my thinking, I drove through the town and out onto the open road. Without a destination, and with muddled thoughts, the journey was pointless. But it wasn't too late yet, I finally realised, executing the worst U turn in the world.

I could see from the crowd dispersing outside the hall that the dance had ended and, at the same time, saw her come out. Lowering the window I called out her name. She turned, an enquiring look on her face, and came over towards the car.

"It's me. John," I said.

The street lighting was poor.

"John Grant," I shouted.

"John Grant," she repeated, in recognition at last.

I scrutinised her features as she came towards me, seeing only the inquisitive look that was to be expected.

"Did you enjoy the dance?" I asked her cheerily.

"I didn't see you there" she replied, a look of surprise on her face. This didn't tell me much either, and I wasn't sure if I should even own up to having been in the hall.

"How's the Pastor?" I asked, to change the subject.

"Dad's fine," she said, smiling softly. "Have you come to see him?"

'Did the smile go with the question?', I wondered. Was she hoping that I had come to see her father and not her, making our meeting friendly and undemanding? If so, things weren't getting any better.

'I've come to see you' was what I wished I could say, but what had there been in her response in these first few minutes that encouraged me to say this?

"Can I give you a lift?" I offered.

"I think I'd better walk," she replied hesitantly, increasing my overall fear of being rejected.

Glancing back in the direction she had come from, she straightened up and waved to someone I could make out in the side view mirror to be her partner at the dance.

"Anybody I know?" I asked, not happy at the appearance of a would-be rival.

"Jim Robertson. No, you won't have met him. He's assisting at the Church," she explained. "A mature student in his last year at University. Could you give him a lift, too?"

I followed her gaze, watching the figure draw nearer until, leaning further out of the car window, I was introduced to him as an old friend.

This was better than just being an old acquaintance, I thought, grasping the friendly hand now being extended to me by a man with neatly combed dark hair and pleasant features.

"Which way are you going?" I asked him, not pleased that I was addressing them as a couple.

Why had I not considered this possibility before? I asked myself as they got into the car. Since I had had no intention of visiting the Pastor on this occasion, the issue that I had come here to settle had seemed straightforward. It was to determine the nature of her feelings for me. But whatever these feelings actually were, might no longer be the sole issue, I could see. What were her feelings, not just for me, but for this other man?

"Second on the right for Jim please," she said politely.

Whatever her relationship was with this man, I couldn't detect anything in the way she spoke to him in the car which might confirm that it was more than friendship. Although they had hardly said anything, I still felt relieved. Even more so, when he got out.

Too soon after that we had stopped outside the Manse. Thanking me for the lift, she caught my eye politely, or was it meaningfully, before she turned towards the gate.

I had to say something. But what? It didn't seem right to ask her for a date. It was too risky at this early stage. It was safer to be a friend rather than a suitor, I decided.

"Church in the morning?" I asked casually.

"Jim's taking the service," she replied, stopping and turning towards me. "Dad will be away."

"Oh right."

"Why don't you come."

So friendship had worked. It wasn't to be the brush off. Far from it. She had taken the initiative. At least in a sense she had. But I had noticed how her eyes had lit up at the mention of the other man's name. This had to be more than just admiration for his speaking ability, more than just friendship, I feared. But no, it didn't have to be, I finally persuaded myself.

"Can I meet you for coffee after the service?" I asked, making the most of the opportunity that had at last come my way.

"I'd like that. Of course you can."

Driving back down through the town, I began to feel good about things, although I knew that since catching that first glimpse of her at the dance I was no further on with regard to how she felt about me. But, and it was the usual big 'but' that the world depended on, things might improve at our next meeting. I would, of course, do my best to see that they did.

But how many times had I said something like this? I asked myself, exasperated. To make the most of an opportunity implied that you had some control over the outcome. But the outcome depended on her feelings, not mine. I had come all this way to find out what these feelings were, not to change them. Meeting her after the service on Sunday wasn't so much an opportunity to make the most of, it was more an occasion on which I was likely to find out if the relationship was going to go any further, or if she was going to become no more than a sad memory, only coming to mind now and then in the picture on the Sales Office wall.

chapter
six

Sitting beside Andy at a corner table in the Old Toll Bar were two young women. I guessed that they would come up to a certain standard as far as their looks went, and I was right.

As I drew nearer I saw that one of them had auburn hair and as she turned and caught my eye in a friendly way I knew instinctively who she was. This was Karen, Andy's girl. With a fair complexion and quite delicate, clearly-defined features, she made a strong impression on me right from the start.

"My friend and colleague, John Grant," Andy informed them, with affected and light-hearted pomposity. The other girl looked up, too, and smiled. "How do you do, John?" she said warmly.

She had short, dark hair, a fuller face than Karen, and was attractive in a different way – pretty too, but slightly less sophisticated.

"What are you having, John?" Andy asked, pushing playfully against the dark-haired girl to make room for me at the table.

"Whisky," I told him, in the clipped tone of a seasoned drinker, hoping that I had got it right.

I was glad to hear Andy coax the dark-haired girl to stay with us for the evening. I had thought at first he might have brought her along secretly to make up a foursome, but apparently not. That I was here, in unfamiliar surroundings, in the company of not just one but two such nice-looking women, surely made me rightly suspicious of my good luck, I told myself, feeling streetwise, as many a seasoned drinker was inclined to be.

"This is Karen," Andy said, in a timely introduction. "And this is Liz".

"So you work beside Andy?" Liz asked me, continuing to smile warmly and directly at me.

"At Bartons, yes."

"I thought you looked too intelligent to work in there", she declared, her apparent bluntness taking me by surprise, but her still warm smile at once taking the edge off the remark.

"Now, Liz," Andy scolded. "John might think you don't like him."

"Here's Steve and Big Tom," Liz then exclaimed, looking towards the doorway.

The big man, walking a little in front of his companion, at first glance seemed chubby, but where a paunch might have been expected I could see there was none, only a broad waistband supported by heavy thighs that bulged through his jeans. He didn't seem in the least bit overweight, just big and heavy.

"Everyone move round three places," Andy ordered light-heartedly.

"Watch it," said Tom, grinning at Andy as he took his seat.

"This is John," Andy said to the two newcomers. "John, this is Steve. You've probably seen him in the workshop, and this is Tom."

"Nice to meet you," said the small, dark-skinned man with a neat build and black, wavy hair. "You're in the sales office, aren't you?"

"John," greeted Big Tom, smiling broadly and extending his hand.

I felt distinctly out of place, although no one was treating me as if I was. They just weren't the kind of people I was used to, although not in the sense that they were any better than my friends at the Food Importers and certainly not in the sense that they were any worse. In fact, I couldn't see anybody looking down on them. But I couldn't quite place them in any social group I had encountered before.

"You think I'm overweight?" I heard Big Tom ask Liz.

"No. You're just well-fed and irresistible" she had replied soothingly.

"You've got it wrong Liz." Steve cut in. "Tom's not an irresistible force, he's an immovable object."

"A bit of both, maybe," Liz answered thoughtfully and then, "So you work beside Andy?" she asked me, repeating her earlier question and turning towards me.

"Well, if you're Andy's friend I suppose you must be OK" she declared.

"I don't like the way you said that," I returned, smiling in what I hoped would seem to be a friendly challenge.

"How did I say it?"

"As if you found it surprising that I'm OK."

"I take it back," she said, putting her arm round my shoulder. "Are we friends? Please."

At once I liked Liz a lot. Strangely, in spite of her forthrightness, there was a gentleness about her that reminded me of Linda, although I supposed she wouldn't have much else in common with her. The thought of Linda sitting at the table drinking whisky was ridiculous. She came from a completely different background, another dimension, a place that I felt, especially right then, was far away and out of my reach.

"Who's for darts?" Big Tom shouted a few rounds later, during which time I had been smiling and nodding enthusiastically, not saying much, but trying my best to fit in.

Darts weren't for me, I realised, as I stood up to join him. Three double whiskies sipped slowly would maybe have been all right but I had gulped them down to keep up with everyone else and to make matters worse the beer had multiplied their effect. I had to sit back down.

"Anybody else?" Tom asked.

"Oh sit down and be quiet," Liz scolded, coming over to sit closer to me.

"We're all pissed", Andy told Tom. "Give the darts a miss tonight big man. Come on. Finish your drink."

Smiling at Andy in agreement, Karen pushed Tom's half empty glass towards its owner.

"And where do you come from with an accent like that?" Liz asked, turning towards me again. "It's nice. Really nice."

"From somewhere else."

"And what are the people like there?" she asked in the same tone. "Are they as nice as us?"

"Nowhere near it," I assured her, with drink-induced enthusiasm.

She punched me playfully. "I like your friend," she said to Andy.

The others laughed and Big Tom leaned over and patted me on the back.

"I like you too," he said. "You're a good bloke."

It felt great that they were treating me like this, even if it was partly due to the effects of the whisky. I knew, of course, that Andy would have played a part in it too. He had probably told them I had passed some very good sales leads to him and that I was all right, a good bloke, as Tom had just said, although I had hoped it was a bit more than that.

Coming from Andy, I knew, as I sat there almost feeling at home now, such an accolade would carry weight. Coming here for a drink with him and meeting his friends had been a success. Not that the Pastor would see it this way, I hazily reflected. Always able to express his disapproval of things in a way that registered, the Pastor had early on given me the clear impression that he thought getting drunk was wrong. I looked about me at my companions who, in spite of this, seemed to be reliable and well-meaning people. Were they all to be assigned to the Pastor's spiritual rubbish heap? I asked myself, irritably.

But I knew in my heart it wasn't as simple as that. Even membership of the Church didn't guarantee anything, the Pastor had once pointed out. On the other hand, allowing membership of the Church to people who plainly, or even not so plainly, didn't subscribe to its basic teachings, undermined its witness and effectiveness, he had contended. And so it was only in a narrow alcohol-related and difficult to understand way that we might not qualify, I concluded, feeling a bit better about things.

That merely 'being born' wasn't sufficient to get you into the Church was another of his pet ideas. As he put it, 'your acts, your disposition and your state with regard to the moral law of God were of crucial importance'. There was a kind of entrance exam to get you in, at least into his one.

"Another drink?" Steve asked.

According to the Pastor, I thought even more hazily, unable to change my subject, a right relationship with God didn't come automatically, as if it was your birthright. And the unrestricted access afforded to the users of a bus shelter shouldn't be thought of as a criteria for admitting new Church members. But if you keep all kinds of people out, I couldn't help asking myself, what did this say about the people you actually let in? Weren't they a bit like the joggers who ran past you, because they were able to? Wasn't an activity of this kind mainly for those who were already fit, and membership of certain churches for those who were already in? That no one could be halfway in or halfway out, according to this way of looking at things was a problem, as I saw it.

*

As Andy waved over to someone and went to speak to them at a nearby table on the other side of the bar he left a gap, that had an almost gravitational pull, beside Karen. As I settled down next to her, I thought she looked even better from close up and that she was absolutely right for Andy, definitely in the same class. They both had something about them.

As she lifted her glass I saw she had thin, well-manicured hands and thin wrists, an observation I felt at home with, one that Andy wouldn't be inclined to object to. When I combined these pleasant rather than exciting features with some of the other things I found appealing about her I began to feel a little uncomfortable. But it still seemed all right to notice that she looked intelligent and capable.

"And where do you come from?" she asked me. "You're not from around here, are you?"

That she had a soft voice and pronounced her words clearly was also a legitimate observation, I knew, but feeling that I was beginning to run out of suitable words to describe Andy's girl.

"You mean my country of origin?"

"Not exactly", she replied, a hint of coldness in her voice.

"I'm only joking," I assured her, aware that my remark seemed to have struck a wrong note. I wanted her to like me, even if it could only be in a certain way, because of Andy. But I wasn't succeeding. She was being far too polite and formal with me. I had to find some way of changing this.

"All right. I'll tell you anything you want to know. In fact, I'll tell you my mother's maiden name, too."

"You don't have to go as far as that," she said, the look on her face telling me that this remark hadn't gone down too well, either. She didn't seem to understand me, not the way Liz did.

"What am I missing?" Andy asked, squeezing back in between us.

"Sorry Andy, I'll need to go," Karen said abruptly, standing up, waving over to Liz, and smiling warmly at Andy.

*

"Enjoying yourself?" Andy asked, putting an arm round my shoulder affectionately, just like Liz had done.

"Very much," I lied cheerily. It would have been the truth, but for the awkwardness with Karen. And she had left at the worst possible moment, just when I had needed to say something that would please her, anything!

"How do you like the crowd?" he asked.

Since my companions, by Pastor Mackenzie's standards, were a bit suspect, I felt I had to assure Andy that I liked his friends. I didn't need to convince myself.

"A great bunch," I told him. "They've taken my mind off things."

"Off fire extinguishers?"

"Off Sears, I suppose."

"He's getting to you?"

"I suppose he is," I admitted reluctantly.

"The world's crawling with people like him," Andy said, looking at me thoughtfully.

"One's enough for me."

"One's more than enough," he returned. "That's if you can't do anything about it."

"How do you mean?"

I sensed he was making a point, something that was cutting across my line of thought, but I wasn't sure what he meant.

"I suppose we could always put a bullet in his head, or something like that," he suggested.

"Good idea," I returned with a conviction I didn't feel happy about. "I maybe wouldn't go quite as far as that," I added quickly, not sure how serious he was.

"Well, maybe not that," he conceded. "But something along those lines. Pressure of some kind or another."

I still wasn't sure if he was serious but I could tell from his manner of speaking that he was much more at home with the idea associated with the bullet than I was.

"Don't worry, John," he said, sensing the shakiness in my response. "It's not a serious consideration, certainly not right now. Come on, drink up."

"And are we going to see more of you?" Liz asked, putting her arm round my shoulder again, reminding me of the light heartedness that had begun to wear off when Karen had left, and which had almost gone as I had tried to come to terms with Andy's remarks.

"You're certainly going to see a lot more of me, I hope" I replied in a loud voice.

"We hope so, too," Tom said, patting me on the back again.

Later, at the flat, my head began to clear a bit, enabling me to look again at the letter from the building society. The threat of repossession remained, undiminished, but my response had changed. Was there really nothing I could do?

The night at the pub had helped to swipe away some of the mental cobwebs. There hadn't seemed to be a glimmer of hope before I went out, but now, I felt strongly inclined to review the situation. Something had just occurred to me.

*

I had only met my Great Aunt Bethea once, or so I had been told, in my early childhood, although she had always sent me a Christmas card.

She was important to me more than I was inclined to admit, being the last of my Grandfather's generation. The family fortune, whatever that actually was, had devolved upon her and although there was apparently no valid reason why this should not have been so, my Aunt Grace had always thought it terrible that absolutely nothing had been passed down to me. She had, however, never suggested that the matter should become a live issue, or that I should give the subject too much thought.

On the contrary, I had grown up with the idea instilled in me that it was best to forget about Great Aunt Bethea and that side of my family, having been assured by Aunt Grace, on this side, that they deserved no better in view of the hinted at and rather hazy withholding of funds, but mainly because they had no real interest in me, anyway. As far as she was concerned they were bloody relatives, not blood relatives, although she herself would never have put it that way.

Because of this, Great Aunt Bethea had become a symbol, rather than a person, sometimes little more than a starting-off point on my occasional attempts to clarify, or was it to improve, my social standing in my mind's eye.

Unfortunately, describing my Great Aunt as upper middle-class seldom did much more for me than to suggest that I had gone down rather than up in the world. It certainly didn't make me feel any happier about where I really belonged right now!

To have failed to visit her over all those years and do so now with the object of borrowing money, didn't seem right, which brought me to that point in my thinking where I felt that no one but Chopin could help. Reaching into the drawer where the works of the artist lay waiting for me, I took out a CD. I hoped that this man, whose soul must have been similar in texture to my own, would provide me with a means of escape from all this mental and emotional turbulence. It wasn't that his music didn't contain these, too, for it could stir up emotions just as strong and vibrant as those which took soldiers into battle, even if it was hard to put a name to them.

As far as I was concerned, there would be no one better in his sphere than Chopin. What he did was of the highest order. I knew I was by no means the only person in the world who thought this, but I felt as if I was. His music could have been written just for me. In man's search for extra-terrestrial intelligence, I had often thought fancifully, maybe I had stumbled on something and that being able to receive something from another world on the Chopinistic wavelength was a great privilege. The fact that his music didn't make such a deep and lasting impression on everyone wasn't something that bothered me, therefore. You either had a built-in receiver or you didn't.

With the piano, alone, as his chosen forte, Chopin's works could be as majestic and complex as a symphony, while the excellence he achieved in combining melody and harmony was seldom to be equalled, far less surpassed. That the composer Liszt, who came a very close second with me and was also adored by millions, could think as highly of this towering figure as I did surely meant that I wasn't just responding like a sophisticated fan of Elvis Presley.

Having managed to separate myself from my problems at that point, 'those earthly miseries that people drag around with them', the effect of the nocturne 'kicked in' and enabled me to make an out of the body entrance into the higher world of knowledge, exactly as Beethoven had once said it would, of course making no mention of wavelengths and receivers, or even transmitters, and only with a very faint suggestion of a transporter.

Unfortunately, as others had found before me, I didn't understand what it was that I was being told by the music. Maybe Beethoven meant higher world of 'being' rather than 'knowledge'. But I didn't care, for I doubted if such knowledge could be of any practical use anyway, other than for the purpose it had just served. No longer was I completely overwhelmed by my problems, no longer overcome by them. Although they were all still there, Chopin had taken much of the venom out of them.

I liked this flat and its half-way position between the two cities. The quality of the landscaped gardens gave it an upmarket look, beyond its true value, its only negative feature being the amount of the mortgage. Occasionally, I would catch a glimpse of one of my neighbours as our cars passed each other going in and out of the estate and a wave to and fro, which I took to signify a kind of mutual respect, would reinforce the foolish but not entirely unmerited feeling I had of living among the right kind of people.

The wrong kind of people, easy enough to recognise, and seldom hard to hear, were better, if at all possible, to be kept away from, I had often concluded, so far to my great relief.

Although it was good to have moved up in the world, it was unwise to make too much of it. Being common or good class were terms to be wary of, although once embarked on the upward journey there wasn't much need to think about it too much. Going up, made whatever you were leaving seem less obnoxious than it was when you might, like me, be on the way back down. Moreover, if the people at the lower end of the social scale were not to be looked down on, then it was hard to understand the headlong rush, on the part of so many people, to get away from them. But the fact that whatever group you came from had to be below the one you ended up in was a popular sentiment I could appreciate.

If I lost this flat then gone were the attractive, well-kept gardens, gone were the right kind of neighbours, and gone was the advantage of living in a secluded estate, where my privacy was ensured and I could stare out, as I was now doing, at a peaceful scene, undisturbed by suspicious looking passers-by or by noisy and arrogant youths wearing baseball caps and re-enacting scenes from their infancy.

But was it realistic to think that Great Aunt Bethea would help me just because my grandfather had been her brother, or were my hopes no more than a manifestation of that not uncommon psychiatric disorder in which I saw myself as a dispossessed heir to a family fortune? I hoped not.

Would blood really be thicker than water? Would she really care? Or rather, should she really care? I might be a Grant on my father's side but what would my mitochondrial DNA say about me? With the so many different maiden names of my mother's mothers, mothers and their ancestors I could be practically anyone. It was maybe just as well that family trees didn't go back too far. If they had, for instance in the case of many of the Jews of Eastern European ancestry I had read about in the Collection, they might have found out that they weren't Jews at all, but descendants of the Khazars, who adopted the Jewish religion in the 8th Century. Since this meant they were much more closely related to the Huns and the Magyars than they were to Abraham, Isaac and Jacob, what might eventually be uncovered about my own point of origin, or anyone else's for that matter? The Book Collection, and genealogy, could sometimes be a mine of a certain kind of useless information, depending on how you looked at it.

But I hoped that Bethea would take me at face value and treat me like a blood relative rather than a hybrid of some kind and wouldn't think too badly of me for asking her for a loan.

I wondered how I should go about it.

chapter
seven

THIS WAS LINDA'S WORLD NOT MINE, I THOUGHT at first as I took my seat at the back of the Church although, in a certain sense, I felt I had a right to be there. Despite my dislike of church services, I no longer possessed that contemporary mindset which thrived on the often shaky assertions made in best selling books on ancient astronauts, ancient civilisations and a several billion year old universe. I definitely wasn't one of those people who failed to occupy the empty seats around me merely because they thought the Biblical account of Creation was only a myth while the Theory of Evolution was a scientific fact. Many of these absentees, according to the Pastor, had been mesmerised into believing that men came from monkeys just because they looked like them and, in spite of the fact, that there was no actual scientific proof of it.

Just like the masses who had attended the Nazi Party rallies, he would go on, these people were happy for various reasons to soak up any suitable, half-baked ideas that came along, confusing as some evolutionists did for example, the development that takes place within a species with the alleged jump from one species to another and by allowing 'mutations' to convince them of how what still hadn't been proved, after all this time, must have happened. No doubt greatly encouraged by the undoubtedly feeble response of much of the religious establishment, the Pastor had conceded, these unbelievers were only too willing to steep their minds in a teaching such as 'The Survival of the Fittest' put forward by Charles Darwin and others in the 19th century, even if they were unlikely to approve of the way it had in recent times been used in Social Darwinism to inspire and justify a long series of racial 'horrors' in which millions of innocent people – men, women and children, had been murdered by the Nazis.

The biblical account of Creation was no more than a fairytale in this scheme of things, the Pastor would lament, not least because the atheistic world view had been adopted by many well-known scientists, too. But the opinion of a scientist wasn't always a scientific opinion and even a scientific opinion wasn't the same as a scientific fact, he would point out. These people had no right to declare that the worm slithering out of the primeval swamp was so important and should be given the credit for so much. Their claim that the creature man no longer had any need of a Creator, whose edicts might impede his progress and rob him of his pleasure was, in the final analysis, no more than wishful thinking, which of course might be said of people on both sides of the argument. The deciding factor seeming to be the product of the emotions rather than the scientific facts. Truly it might be said that the heart has its reasons that reason know nothing about, I felt I could add, in my often assumed role these days, as an amateur philosopher.

And so I felt I had every right to be sitting there in the Church because, after listening to all this and giving it a lot of thought, I was beginning to direct the universal question, 'How could you believe all that nonsense?' at the unbelievers as well as the believers. Pastor Mackenzie had made a definite impression on me, even if it was only up to a certain point.

In another sense, however, I felt I didn't belong here in the Church. As I rose to my feet to sing the opening hymn, a glance at the first words of the first verse, which I couldn't identify with, seemed to be apt evidence of it. The words, and having to stand up and sing them, made me feel like someone else, someone I didn't want to be.

I didn't enjoy church music, or even music associated with other religions. Congregations bellowing out hymns on television, choir boys on CD singing like angels, and monks chanting in a minor key, all seemed to me to be missing the mark. Hadn't someone in The Book Collection once said that people only painted pictures of Christ when they had lost the real and vital impression of him in their hearts, an observation which I felt quite happy about because I could it use an excuse for my wishy-washy outlook.

To complicate things, although the difference between belief and unbelief didn't ultimately seem to be an intellectual matter, it was still easy to cast doubts on much of what the Pastor had to say. According to him, only one person of stature in history had claimed to teach the absolute truth, to be one with God, and to prove his divine mission by doing works only God could perform. Wasn't it highly unlikely, he would ask, that Christ was an imposter. How could he have got away with such an act for so long and on such a scale? And how could someone like him have been trying to deceive people anyway? What about the perfectly consistent holiness of his life? What about the unwavering confidence with which he challenged investigation of his claims and, not least, what about the fact that he staked everything on the result?

But strongly impressing you with obvious but neglected facts like these was seldom enough for the Pastor. Wasn't it a vast improbability, too, he would go on, that someone like Christ could have lived a lifelong lie in the avowed interest of the truth, and an even greater improbability that such deception could have brought such blessing to the world?

Couldn't Christ have been kidding himself, I had once clumsily suggested. But no. The Pastor had an answer for this too. If Christ was self-deceived it would argue a folly amounting to positive insanity, would it not, while his whole life and character exhibited a calmness, a dignity, an equipoise, and a self-mastery that were utterly inconsistent with this? Or perhaps, even worse, if he was self-deceived surely this would argue a self-ignorance and a self-exaggeration which could only spring from the deepest moral perversion, while the humility of his spirit and the self-denying goodness of his life would make such an assertion incredible.

But surely all this, the parts I could digest, had been ably refuted in various ways for a long time. Hadn't Hitler for example, even far outside his adoring immediate circle and outside his own country, according to one of the books in the Collection, been very successful in getting away with his act, too. In 1935 he had taken in the British Foreign Secretary, and the League of Nations Secretary. In 1937 he had taken in Lord Halifax, in 1938 the British Prime Minister, and in addition to these, a procession of distinguished visitors, including even the famous Lloyd George. Perhaps if he had won the war, posterity would have been taken in by him, too. Or was I stretching the comparison a bit too far, and even in a hopelessly inappropriate direction?, I felt obliged to ask myself.

The Pastor also seemed to have assumed that Christianity had brought great blessing to the world.

'What blessing?' I knew the unbelievers could ask with ease. 'I want nothing to do with organised religion in any of its forms,' they would declare. 'It leads to nothing but wars, pain, and suffering.' But they had got that wrong too, according to the Pastor. It was 'religious' people who had opposed Christ. And the unbelievers had missed the point about religion in general for where it had been dispensed with altogether, in recent times, a lot of people had become surplus to requirement, too. The Inquisition and the Crusades were bloody, but they weren't in the same league as the atrocities committed by the atheist Joseph Stalin and others in more recent times.

After listening to Pastor Mackenzie I now thought that these unbelievers were wrong. But they thought with equal enthusiasm, and often with higher IQs and degrees and doctorates, that they were right, whilst those who genuinely couldn't make up their minds thought the practices of both believers and unbelievers were merely 'life-scripts' rather than absolute truths.

Intellect certainly wasn't what decided whether you believed what the Pastor taught or whether you didn't. It seemed that the unbeliever and the Pastor could both say to each other, prove it, to equal effect.

*

Jim Robertson, the man at the dance, knew how to conduct a service. If he was a rival for Linda's affections then he had a head start on me. He was good at something she liked and, if church people stuck together, as they were inclined to do, what chance did I have?

As I entered the coffee room, her welcoming smile did little to raise my spirits for I knew it would look just as appealing to most of the people there. Was I sharing the smile with them, or were they sharing the smile with me?

Her large brown eyes at once caught me in their spell and her well-shaped lips and faultless complexion did the rest. I hoped it was true that not all beautiful women preferred to be friendly with men who were equally as good to look at.

Was being 'quite' good with women, which was the very best light in which I could see myself, going to be enough. Or, as a 'quite' man, was I hopelessly out of my class?

"Where on earth have you been?" she asked me, at once further deflating my self-confidence, as she joined me at the table.

"You mean …?"

"Since you left."

"Nowhere special," I told her weakly, taken aback by the boldness of her question.

"Secret?" she asked, mischievously, which wasn't like her, I felt.

"No, uneventful," was all I could manage at first.

"Boring?"

"Not boring – unpleasant or rather, unsuccessful."

She had taken the initiative, I could see. And worse, her manner was light-hearted, which unfortunately might mean that the matter wasn't too important to her. But at least she wasn't talking about the Church.

"Unsuccessful at what?" she challenged.

"At what I've been doing."

"And what was that?"

"Sorry Linda, I know I'm being a bit vague," I confessed,

looking for a way to slow her down. I had come here to bring things out into the open, but not as quickly as this. Her questions were too direct. Finally I realised what should have been obvious to me from the start. I still owed her an apology.

"I'm sorry I didn't tell you I was leaving," I said, in a subdued tone.

"You didn't really have to," she answered, avoiding my eyes, awkwardly.

I struggled to find the best answer to this. Did her uneasiness indicate that her feelings for me had been such that my sudden departure had meant something, after all? Did it indicate that she thought there had been something important between us – or was she uneasy at my suggestion of this, because there hadn't been?

"Jim's a good speaker," I blurted out pointlessly.

"A very good speaker," she agreed, nodding in approval.

"Is he a close friend?"

"He certainly is. Well, in a way."

This wasn't clarification – at least not the kind I was looking for.

"We're together quite a lot," she added.

"You mean in Church work?" I asked hopefully.

"Of course. Church work."

I thought, and hoped for some reason, that I could detect a note of impatience in her answer. But I knew I had to change the subject, in case I said the wrong thing.

"Would you like another coffee?" was the best I could manage and then, "Can I give you a run home?" I asked, before she had time to answer the first question. I wasn't handling this very well at all.

*

I drew up outside the Manse and turned in my seat to face her. Pushing open the car door she hesitated, as if about to say something.

"I really am sorry that I never came to see you before I left," I said, repeating my apology.

"You didn't really owe me an explanation, John."

"I still feel bad about it, Linda."

"Why should you?"

Her face was expressionless. Like her tone of voice, it gave nothing away to guide me in my answer. Did this mean that she saw nothing important enough for me to regret, or was her question posed, as I hoped, to get me to define what I thought the relationship had been?

"If I had left in a sensible fashion we could have kept in touch," I said at last.

"You wanted to keep in touch?"

"Was I wrong" I asked, unintentionally being too bold.

"Wrong?"

"I mean, should we have kept in touch?"

"I'm not sure it should be up to me to answer a question like that" she said unexpectedly, throwing me completely off balance.

"Have I said the wrong thing?"

"In a way, maybe," she returned.

Her words were almost enough for me. In a way 'I hadn't said the wrong thing' was what they meant too.

"Would you have liked me to write to you?" I asked her, pressing on hopefully.

"Of course I would," she said firmly.

"You would have been genuinely pleased to hear from me?"

"Of course I would," she repeated.

Was this, at last, what I had come all this way to hear? She would have been genuinely pleased to hear from me. On the other hand, was I putting too much emphasis on the word 'genuine'?

'Genuinely pleased, Linda?" I enquired, trying to keep calm.

"All right. Are you asking me if I missed you? I missed you," she told me, raising her voice slightly.

Did she mean she missed me in the sense that friends miss each other, or even colleagues? I asked myself. I didn't think she did. But I was asking too many questions. Surely enough had been said to make my journey worthwhile. She hadn't rebuffed me. Her response confirmed that she was willing to consider taking up the relationship again, and that these friendly conversations I had had with her, after the services, had meant something to her, too. She hadn't seen me merely as an acquaintance with a common interest in the Church. But to what extent did her feelings for me actually go beyond this?

As she pushed on the car door I caught her arm.

"Have you got to go in? I was thinking we might go for a drive."

"I have to help with the lunch," she answered, apologetically.

My spirits fell at this. How easy it would still be for her to get rid of me.

"Could you come to the Bible Study this evening?" she asked. "Or maybe we could go for a drive some other time," she suggested.

"Could you give me your current phone number?" I asked, my hopes revived.

I drove off in good spirits, leaving the slip of paper with her phone number on it lying on the passenger seat as evidence of the success of the visit.

chapter
eight

I PARKED IN A STREET WHICH HAD ROW UPON ROW
of small shops on each side. Although I lacked conviction, and
experience, I didn't feel incapable. But was I capable enough?
This particular job wasn't like anything I had ever had to do
at the Food Importers and I wished I didn't have to do it.
But Sears had insisted and, anyway, I very much needed the
commission.

To walk in, uninvited, and try to sell someone a fire
extinguisher, or anything else for that matter, was known as
'cold calling'. For this you had to be sensitive, so that you could
detect a buying signal, and insensitive, so that you wouldn't
be too upset when people were rude to you or otherwise
unmoved by your sales overture.

The opposite of 'cold calling' was when someone came to
you with the idea of buying already in their mind. Although
this wasn't referred to as 'hot calling', it was hotly pursued, by
a certain kind of salesmen, as a congenial way of making a

sale. Real salesmen were said to hold anyone in contempt who tried to claim the credit for making a sale through 'hot calling'. Taking an order, which was all it was, according to them, didn't make you a salesman and if they were right my sense of identity was under serious threat again, and I had some hard work ahead of me.

Sears had set the minimum target for this endeavour at two extinguishers a day. For once he had got it right. If I could sell two models worth £200, five days a week, at ten percent commission, plus what I made in the office, it would bring my earnings up to just about what I needed to make ends meet.

I got out of the car, overcoming the temptation to remain sitting there behind the wheel, in that sheltered little world in which I could feel that my strength was adequate, and my integrity intact.

"Don't need any," the sales prospect behind the counter in the first shop told me.

If there was a difference, as it said in the Sales Manual, between what was needed, and what was wanted, the man's harsh tone of voice and challenging look blurred the distinction. But his meaning was clear.

At the next shop, an elderly woman gave me a better reception.

"Sorry, but we bought one last month."

I warmed to her smile. Some people were better than others at delivering bad news, I thought gratefully.

Noting down the street number of each subsequent shop I visited, to monitor my progress or to avoid becoming disorientated, I wasn't sure which, I at last, at the thirty-first shop, met with a response that raised my hopes.

"Are you from the Fire Department?" the woman asked, when I told her the kind of free advice I was offering her about putting out fires.

"We're more or less the same," I lied. "Anything to do with fire extinguishers is our speciality," I added, sprinkling a dash of truth on the falsehood.

"Could you take a look at this one? she asked.

Peering at the extinguisher, I prodded and caressed it hoping that, in her eyes, my demeanour would transcend that of a mere salesman. I was a professional person, brim full of technical expertise.

"It's not in very good condition," I pronounced.

"Will it work?"

"I doubt it."

"What should I do?"

That she should get the extinguisher serviced was the right advice. For a mere twenty pounds or so it could be put back in good working order. To replace it with an absolutely new extinguisher would be an awful lot more than that.

"If I were you, I would get rid of it," I advised her, "and buy a new one."

"It's definitely no good?"

"I'm afraid not," I lied again, looking about the shop as if assessing the fire risk but actually allaying my feelings of guilt.

There was far more at stake for me in this encounter than there was for her, I thought, in an attempt to justify my dishonesty. Her livelihood wasn't under threat, mine was.

"I can let you have something with a very good discount," I offered.

"You mean a new one?"

"One of the very best models."

"How much are they?"

"£220 actually," I said in a measured tone. "But, let me see, £200 after the introductory discount has been applied."

"£200," she gasped.

"It's the very best of equipment."

I knew what her answer was going to be. A pleasant-looking woman, she was staring at me sympathetically. If this had been the first shop, or even the twentieth, I might have put up some resistance to her refusal, definitely offered her a bigger discount, but at the thirty-first shop I was sick of he sound of my own voice.

This job had nothing gong for it, I could see. In the Food Importers the current had seemed to flow in the right direction, the sales prospects had actually wanted what you were selling. In this job it was hard just to stay afloat. Being greeted by assistants who weren't authorised to buy was as bad as being snubbed by owners who were determined not to. It all added up to the same thing, no sale.

Feeling like a survivor heading for the fort, I hoped a long lunch hour in the car would aid my recovery. Trying to get people to buy was like changing the world in miniature, I thought, as I unwrapped my sandwiches. Most of these people neither needed nor wanted a fire extinguisher, and it would take a lot more than evangelistic fervour to get them to buy one. But a lot more what?

I dozed for twenty minutes or so until I was wakened by the rain hammering on the roof of the car. My feet were cold and a strong wind was blowing. Looking across the street, the row of shops I was about to visit looked dull and uninviting.

How many people who worked in sales were real salesmen? I reflected again, with ill-humour. Sitting in warm offices taking phone calls, or in showrooms greeting someone already thinking of buying, these sales people were lulled into thinking that they knew the name of the game. They didn't.

To close the sale was at the pinnacle of their endeavours, was what it was all about, they would proclaim, as would the pundits and the sales manuals.

But they were all wrong. There was another kind of salesman, salesmen who were predators first, who had to prowl, stalk, and pursue, salesmen who had to do all this before the skills of persuasion necessary to closing the sale could even be brought into play.

And yet, cold calling, which consisted of this aggressive and creative approach lacked prestige. The cold-caller, made in the mould of the explorer and the adventurer, was often employed and supervised by people of lesser stamp, who loved to lord it over them and pontificate on the difficulties encountered along the way, a job that they, themselves, shrunk from because they had neither the personality nor the stamina to do it. It looked as though I wasn't going to be able to make the grade, either.

I had visited thirty-one shops, pleaded with more or less thirty-one people, and I hadn't sold a thing. As far as my quality of life was concerned, I felt like someone who had just begun a long prison sentence. But wasn't I a kind of prisoner already? I asked myself.

I needed something stronger than tea, at that point but, having to resist the urge, I reached for my flask. I was two extinguishers short of my target. How many shops was this going to take?

The street had now become busy with shoppers, I noticed, their purpose so very different from mine. They wanted to buy and I wanted to sell. There wouldn't be anyone here for the same reason that I was. I was in a kind of 'solitary'.

I was a prisoner to my thoughts too, filled with self-recrimination for getting into this situation. If only I could have lost my job at the Food Importers through redundancy and become an object of pity, a victim of some economic downturn, I would have felt better about things. If I had been a redundant 'square tube fitter' forced to learn new skills elsewhere as a 'circular tubeless turner', I would have felt no self-reproach in my plight, and a redundancy payment might have reduced my overdraft and raised my spirits.

But to have been propelled into a situation like this by behaviour that was ill-timed and out of character, was bad. I hadn't even been caught in the act. The boss at the Food Importers hadn't walked into the ante room and caught her with her panties at her ankles. The situation, and her state of undress, certainly hadn't gone nearly as far as that. And from what I had heard, his behaviour at the dance hadn't been much better than mine. Could I honestly say that I deserved to be in this situation?

But did it matter whether I deserved it or not? I had let my guard drop and this is where it had got me, sitting here in the car contemplating endless rows of shops whose occupants lurked inside waiting to reject me.

Reduced to my recollections centred on panties that I had never seen, far less removed, and faced with the prospect of an afternoon that would be much like the morning, I struggled to resist the despair that was overcoming me.

What was I up against in this business?, I reflected bitterly. Judging from the number of fire extinguishers in the country, the small fires they were meant to put out seemed to pose a greater threat than Hell's fire itself.

If even one small fire was lit for every extinguisher that existed there's no doubt the country would go up in flames. But the vast majority of them would be bought, installed and discarded without seeing any action. There were ten times more extinguishers in the land than there were six shooters in the Wild West. The country was infested with them. And yet I was expected to sell only two a day, three if I was good, and I couldn't even sell one.

And wasn't there something undignified about forcing

yourself on people in this way? And even if I did sell one, would it be enough to make any real difference to my overall situation?

There would be something undignified about seeking help from my Great Aunt, too, I reflected dismally, but again, what real alternative did I have. I had to do something, whether I liked the idea or not. Things were going from bad to worse. She might be my last chance.

chapter
nine

IN THE PUB CAR PARK I TOOK OFF MY TIE AND
pulled out the neck of my shirt so that it hung over the collar
of my jacket, not sure if it would be enough to change my
image, but determined to make the effort. I wanted to fit in. I
wanted to at least look as if I belonged in the place.

Karen was sitting by herself and greeted me, without
a smile! unsurprisingly, of course, in view of the low point
reached in our last conversation.

"And what kind of work do you get up to?" I asked her, to
dispel the awkward silence.

"I work at the Casino," she replied. "Mainly in the office."

"And you enjoy it?" I asked, wishing I could have thought
of something impressive or exciting to say instead.

"I like the money."

"I suppose casinos pay well?"

"I suppose they do."

I was doing my best to reach her, but a series of questions, all mine, didn't amount to the kind of conversation I wanted to have with her. She was Andy's girl. I wanted to get along with her.

"I can't say the same about Fire Protection," I told her. "Just the opposite, as far as the money goes."

"So I've heard," she commented, turning to face me. "Did you know Andy before you came here?" she asked me unexpectedly. It was something I thought she would have known.

"Only in Bartons."

"Well John, aren't you going to buy me a drink?" she asked, pleasantly surprising me with the request, and with her use of my first name. On the other hand, she could hardly have addressed me as Mr Grant. Still, things seemed about to improve?

"Of course I am," I said hastily. "What would you like?"

"Orange juice."

"Orange juice?" I repeated, not sure if she was serious.

"Yes, with some gin in it, of course," she added with a smile.

There was something about the way her lip curled up at one side, even before she smiled, that made a strong impression on me. It wasn't just the attractiveness of the feature that held my attention, it was its familiarity, and yet I had only met her once before. It was as if I had somehow known I was going to meet someone like her at some point in my life. I couldn't make too much of this, of course, because of Andy, but I found it hard to shake the idea.

"I don't think you feel at home in here, do you?" she asked pleasantly, fingering her glass.

"I don't?"

"I think you feel you're too good for the place," she said, with a forthrightness that caught me completely unawares.

"I do actually," I stated, trying to look as if I meant it and seeing at once, from her puzzled look, that I had succeeded.

"Don't you agree?" I teased, further.

"If you say so."

"You surely don't think I'm serious," I asked, worried that I might have gone too far.

"I'm not quite sure what to think," she replied, her features shaped in mock disapproval. And then, in a lighter tone, "But since you once told me to mind my own business..."

"Surely I didn't say that?" I protested. You must have misunderstood me."

"I was hurt about your mother's maiden name too," she stated, feigning a look of teenage petulance which I felt was significant. The ice was definitely melting.

"Ask me anything you want to," I told her. "What would you like to know?"

"Mmm. Let me see," she murmured. "Now that you're volunteering the information, did you leave anyone behind when you came here?"

"You mean family or ..."

"Not quite," she broke in, raising her eyebrows knowingly.

I liked the fact that at last the conversation was coming to life, but immediately felt uneasy about the direction in which it was going. What could I tell her about Linda? I wasn't even sure if Linda was the answer to her question. I hadn't left her behind, not in the way she meant.

"There was someone," I told her, against my better judgement.

"Can I ask her name?"

"Linda."

"Will I be likely to meet her?"

"You might," I lied. "Maybe not in here though."

I was glad to see Andy come in, hopeful that he might once more be bringing with him a change of subject.

"Where did you say your flat was, John?" he asked me when he had settled.

"Castle Bridge, Andy. A good central point for the whole region."

"Castle Bridge," he repeated thoughtfully. "Expensive, surely?"

"It is."

"Mortgaged?"

"Yes."

"How can you afford if off what Sears pays you?" he inquired, sounding surprised.

I hesitated. This was a possible juncture in my relationship with them. Since Karen had gone to the ladies, I wondered if should tell him about my plight.

"The truth is, Andy, right now I can't pay for it," I told him, smiling awkwardly, and wishing I hadn't said it.

"You mean ..."

"Things are bit tight," I said, trying to sound as if the matter was under control, and hoping I hadn't already given the game away.

"To what extent, John?"

"I'm running a few months behind, I suppose."

"How much do you need?", he asked, counting off some notes from a long brown envelope he had taken out of his inside jacket pocket.

"Two hundred pounds," I gasped. "Andy, you're joking?"

"It isn't a problem, John . Go on, take it." he coaxed "or do you need a bit more?"

"Two hundred pounds, Andy," I repeated, running the notes through my hand.

"John, I'm into good money right now, very good money. You can pay me back when things improve. Go on. Don't worry about it," he said, grinning, as if it didn't matter, and winking at me as Karen rejoined us.

Andy and his girlfriend were both having a profound effect on me. They were spontaneous and sincere, people I could respect. Everything about them was stimulating, so different from what I had had to put up with recently, so different from the overall set of circumstances which was almost bringing me to my knees. Andy was for me, when everything else seemed to be against me, and Karen was putting the spring back in my step, or something like that.

And so was Liz, I thought, as the slim, dark-haired girl joined us.

"I suppose you'll all be coming back to my place tonight?" she asked as Karen and Andy smiled and raised their glasses in assent.

"What about you, John?" she asked.

"You mean a party of some sort?"

*

Liz's flat would be around half the price of my own, I calculated as we turned into the street. Although the tenement building was solid-looking, the name plates at the entrance had the residents' names written in biro and stuck on with tape in typical down-market fashion.

"Oh no, not him again," Liz said, as we walked ahead of the others, pointing to a figure outlined in the doorway.

"Someone you know?" I asked her.

"No, I don't," she said irritably. "That's the trouble with city centre living, people like him are always hanging about, which can be worrying, especially when the security door is left unlocked.

The man moved to one side to let us pass and stared at us

insolently. Unshaven and unwashed, with crumpled clothing, he looked the part.

As the security door clicked shut behind us I felt I should have challenged the man, although an encounter of this kind wasn't something I felt happy about. With my quite respectable and educated appearance, it would be only too obvious that I wasn't an expert in the martial arts. Soon, however, I felt that such a passive response wouldn't do. It didn't feel or look good.

"Do you want me to say something to him?" I ventured.

"No. What's the use," Liz lamented, glancing back down the stairs with a disapproving look on her face. "The problem is we're far too near the city centre," she repeated. "What happens is, you contact the police, spend half an hour waiting on them to arrive and a further half hour giving them your name and address, even your age believe it or not, and end up wishing you hadn't bothered phoning them."

I thought of my own quiet estate and the likelihood of having to move from it, probably into a district not unlike this one, even worse. It would be hard to take.

"Besides," Liz went on, "you don't really know who you're dealing with. Most of these people are harmless, even in need of help, but you can never tell."

"I'll shift him," I found myself saying. She called my name several times, disapproving of my action, as I went back down to the entrance. Pulling open the security door apprehensively, but with a flourish, I stepped outside.

The man had moved away from the doorway, just as Big Tom and Steve were arriving, followed by Andy a few yards behind.

"Going home already John?" Steve asked good-humouredly. I pointed at the bedraggled figure now moving slowly away from us down the street.

"He's annoying Liz," I explained boldly, still determined to save face. "Always hanging about."

Big Tom took his hands out of his pocket and stared in the man's direction, his eyes narrowing and the expression on his face becoming deadly serious.

"Let me do it, Tom" Steve said, catching his arm. "I need the exercise."

"What's the problem?" Andy asked as he came up.

"Him. He's been annoying Liz. Always hanging about," Steve told him, pointing down the street. "I'm going to have a word with him."

"OK, but take it easy. Remember, we're going to a party."

I watched Steve saunter up to the man as if he was about to ask for directions.

"Piss off," I heard him say, indicating an attitude not in keeping with what I considered to be the received wisdom in such matters. But whether the man was harmless or dangerous, homeless, or on drugs, or fluctuated between these, were things that Steve didn't seem to think were relevant.

"Go on. Piss off," I heard him say again.

The man was half a head taller than Steve and looked much heavier. He pulled himself up to his full height and glowered down at him.

In one dynamic movement, as if pushing a boulder over a cliff, Steve drove his shoulder into the man's chest, driving him back against the wall of the building.

The man stood there for an instant, his eyes bulging, glaring at Steve, and then, without retaliating or even uttering a word of protest, he made off down the street.

"Don't come back," Steve shouted after him.

I wondered what would have happened if the others hadn't come along when they had. Steve had certainly got me off the hook. He had taken the complexity out of the situation in a way that I could never have done.

It wasn't just that I was filled with admiration for what he had done although, from an immediate practical point of view, I certainly was. My exhilaration was more expansive than that. I realised that being in their company was doing me the world of good. It was revitalizing my depleted outlook on life. It was boosting my morale to see that there were other ways of solving problems than the ones I was used to. Maybe it was only some trivial gap in my knowledge or understanding that was holding me back. Maybe it wasn't too late to put things right. In the light of all this, maybe going to see Aunt Bethea wasn't such a bad idea. I had to look at all the angles, didn't I?

"Now let's get to this party," Steve said, as he rejoined us.

He looked as unruffled as Big Tom who stood beside me, his hands in his pockets, the taut look gone from his face. It seemed that I was the only one who would need to calm down.

*

Among the guests, Liz told me as we went in, were the couple who lived downstairs. As the amplified music from the CD player blared its accompaniment to the raised voices of the partygoers, I hoped, for their own sake, that the other neighbours had been invited too.

I could see that the first room we came to had been rearranged, with most of the furniture pressed against the walls to make space for the dancing. The other public room, into which I was taken by Liz, had been converted into a lounge bar, with various kinds of tables dotted about in it. A dining-room table, loaded with bottles and glasses, stood at the far end.

Spotting a vacant corner table, I poured myself a lager and made my way over to watch the guests arriving. Most of them were couples, who smiled and nodded at me as they went past and I could see that Liz's friends were, just like she herself was, not too sophisticated, but friendly and respectable, and that the party would reflect this, although noisily so.

The lager settled nicely on top of what I had drunk in the pub and I responded enthusiastically when Liz placed a hand on each of my shoulders and pushed and steered me down the hall into the other room, where she soon had me wiggling and jerking my body in unison with her own.

When the music changed she broke away from me for an instant, returning to encourage me into more energetic movements, by pulling and pushing my arms and body.

The effort I made to succeed in this taxed me, but I persevered, anxious to gain her approval. When at last the music stopped I collapsed breathless onto a chair, feeling that I had acquitted myself well.

"You're quite good at this," she said to me, confirming that my efforts had been successful.

At all costs I wanted to be accepted, and I was beginning to feel that I was succeeding in this.

What I liked about Liz I knew others would like too, and she was soon snatched away from me by Big Tom, whose huge frame she seemed just as anxious to control. They looked good together and it occurred to me I might have to be just as careful with them, in this respect, as I was with Karen and Andy. Discreetly deciding to get out of the way I went through to the other room and sat at a table behind the door, basking in my success at this kind of dancing. I felt relaxed and in good spirits, glad that the universal cry of "let's have a party' had such a sound psychological basis. I thought it a great pity that, just like listening to Chopin, the therapeutic content of party-going dealt with effects, rather than causes.

I wondered what Linda would think if she could see me now, or the Pastor for that matter. Social events of this kind would be disapproved of in the Church, where forbidden practices seemed to grow in number, so that gradually the combined force they exerted became greater than the ability required to fully understand their significance, and even when they were fully understood, to get emotionally adjusted to them.

I thought once more of the services I had attended, singing hymns that had expressed ideas I couldn't appreciate, while the sound of the church organ had made me thankful for the existence of Chopin. His music was written for people like myself. The church music wasn't. I wasn't sure about the sounds coming from the amplifier.

My light-heartedness began to slip away and I felt annoyed at myself for letting thoughts like this intrude into my party-going. I didn't need reminding that the Food Importers wasn't all I had been troubled by before coming here.

But I was now facing a set of circumstances that were proving to be just as bad. Up to my eyes in debt and in danger of losing the flat, my ability to sell fire extinguishers seemed to equate with my ability to survive.

"Thought you had run away," Andy said, poking his head round the door, just in time to pull my thoughts out of their downward spiral.

"From what?"

"I saw you dancing with Liz."

There was something about Andy that didn't add up, I couldn't help thinking, as I remembered the wad of notes I had seen bulging out of the envelope. But it wasn't only that. Telling people they needed another fire extinguisher when they didn't, or that the one they owned was the wrong kind when it wasn't, didn't seem to be an occupation that was worthy of him. He didn't seem to belong in Bartons any more than I did myself.

"Liz's great company, isn't she?" he commented.

"Hard to keep up with."

"Karen can be great too, but she takes longer to get to know," he told me.

"She was telling me about her job."

"Oh yes. At the Casino. I sometimes work for them too," he said ponderously.

"Doing what, Andy?" I asked, puzzled.

"A driver of sorts. Would you be interested in that kind of thing?" he asked me.

"In being a driver?"

"A courier, actually," he said, looking at me questioningly. "Part-time, of course, usually in the evenings or at weekends, but it pays very well. Very well indeed."

So I had been right. Andy was more than a fire extinguisher salesman. But what was he?

"All you do is deliver things," he explained, "packages for the most part. Quite often to caravans, which are dotted about here and there."

"Packages of what Andy?"

"They won't be radioactive, if that's what you mean," he said, grinning good-naturedly.

Andy was doing me another favour. He was inviting me further into his world, whatever that was. And anyway, didn't postmen deliver packages without knowing what was in them?

"Sounds interesting, Andy," I replied in an understatement. "Could I give it a try?" How could I say anything else? Hadn't I decided to look at all the angles? "I'll fill you in on the details later on," he said. "There's always work of this kind in the offing."

chapter
ten

Aunt Bethea's house had three storeys and looked as big as several two-bedroom semis. It had windows in the attic and basement, too, the ones on the ground floor being huge, with those on the two upper storeys looking only a little less imposing. I was glad there was a sturdy big hedge at the foot of the driveway. This would prevent anyone in the house seeing me parked there, peering up at the house.

I sat for a while looking about me, surprised that a district like this still existed so near the centre of the city. The houses were all in good repair and the gardens well kept. In many other cities big, old houses such as these would probably have been converted into flats, offices, or small hotels but here residents with private means or big salaries had obviously found it congenial to stay on.

I felt ashamed that I was making this visit basically because she was rich and I was poor. The fact that I was only a year or so away from a family kitty in which I might have had a share didn't give me a right to be here.

I had finally got as far as I had by acting on impulse, without phoning my Great Aunt to tell her I was coming. I had no idea what kind of reception awaited me.

In spite of the reason for my visit, I cared about the impression I would make on her. I wanted her to think that I was a worthy bearer of the family name – a quality, I remembered from the Book Collection, that had once been wished prayerfully on his children, not without some success, by the father of Bernard Montgomery one of the most famous British Field Marshals in the Second World War. I supposed it was even possible that my own father had wished something like this on me and I wondered if this was why I wasn't finding it easy to play the part of the poor relation looking for a hand-out.

But that's what I was here for, so what was the best way to go about it? I asked myself. 'I was wondering if there was any possibility that you might be able to lend me some money', didn't sound too good, although it came right to the point. Needless to say, I wished at that moment, from the bottom of my heart, that I could get the loan somewhere else.

Tidying my hair in the car mirror and straightening my tie, I got out and made my way up the driveway.

"Is Miss Grant at home?" I asked the robust looking, elderly woman who confronted me in the doorway.

"Is it something personal, or …?"

"I'm a relative. Could you tell her a John Grant has called to see her?"

"Oh, a Mr Grant. Could you wait for just a minute?" the woman asked me, her scrutinising glare becoming a polite look of curiosity.

Alone in the doorway, I felt my nervousness subside. The

name on the door was my name. I had a kind of right to be here, I told myself foolishly, almost believing it.

On the other hand, I reflected pessimistically, Aunt Bethea might not see me as a Grant at all. She might think I was more of a McCutcheon, which was my mother's maiden name, and of course Grace's too. I felt my nervousness return.

My mind went blank as the woman led me down a broad well-carpeted hallway and ushered me into a room at the far end where a thin-faced old woman was sitting at a window with some knitting on her lap. She looked up as I went in, motioning me to a nearby chair, while the other woman left the room, closing the door gently behind her.

The old lady, my Great Aunt, put her knitting down and looked across at me.

"So you're George's boy," she said thoughtfully. "Yes, you look like him," she added, a kindly smile appearing on a face that I thought I had seen before. Her features were heavily wrinkled and topped by thick, quite long, grey hair. She looked very much as I had imagined her – ladylike, and her high cheekbones and long face were features I then remembered seeing in photographs of my father.

"This is a lovely house," I commented politely.

"You like it, then?" she said, smiling with her eyes too now.

"I certainly do."

"But you've been here before," she told me.

"I have?" I was genuinely unsure if I should remember.

"Of course you have," she said gently.

"I've absolutely no recollection of it."

"No. You'd be too young to remember, but you used to come here often when you were a toddler," she informed me.

She was the kind of old woman I liked, petite and with a dignified posture apparent in the way she was sitting. Her voice, although soft, was still quite firm and clear. The passage of time had deftly etched the many wrinkles on her forehead and cheeks making it easy to see that she would have been very pleasant to look at in her younger days. It felt good to be related to someone like her.

"And what has brought you here after all these years?" she asked me.

"I was wondering if ...," I began in accordance with my script, my throat parched. But the prepared words of my request for a loan wouldn't come.

"I was wondering if I might be able to find out something about this side of my family," I said instead, feeling the tension within me subside.

"You did, did you?" she chided gently. "You've taken an awful long time to get round to it, haven't you? But better late than never, I suppose."

From the window I could see that bushes and trees were obscuring the view the occupants of the neighbouring houses would have of the back garden. This was living in the city graciously, without being hemmed in too much and overlooked. If only there could have been something equally gracious about my reason for being here, I thought guiltily.

"Well, there's a good place to start," she said, in answer to my question about my family, pointing to a small picture hanging beside a standard lamp in a nearby corner of the room.

"Go on," she coxed. Move the lamp back and have a look."

The picture was of a middle-aged man with dark reddish hair and beard.

"It's an original," she said.

"Is it someone I should know?"

"That's your great great grandfather," she told me. "You're not unlike him, even without the beard."

"Do you think so?" I asked enthusiastically, intrigued by the observation.

"In fact, you're very like him," she confirmed, her eyes going rapidly from my face to the picture and back again a few times. "You're a Grant all right, at least to look at. There's no doubt about it."

I smiled self-consciously, delighted by her affirmation.

Could this refined old lady really have robbed me of an inheritance? I asked myself. Did the version of events given to me over the years by Aunt Grace really paint an accurate picture of what had happened? Had my Great Aunt Bethea alone got what I should have at least had a small share of? I felt, now that I was here with her, that it didn't seem likely. It wasn't as if I had had a claim to the throne, anyway. I had only been second or third in line. Grace had been making too much out of my position perched, by her way of it, on a branch quite high up on the family tree. I was also perched quite low down too. It depended on how you looked at it, or who you were.

"And what about your career?" she asked me, leaning forward in her chair a little.

"I'm in Fire Protection. I sell fire extinguishers."

"Fire extinguishers?" she repeated, looking at me strangely for a moment. "Well I could do with a fire extinguisher. Can you get discounts for people you know?" she asked, surprising me with her worldliness.

"I'll get you one at cost price," I told her, glad of the opportunity to express the warm family feeling that was welling up inside me. I felt really pleased that after so many years of separation from the family whose name I bore, I was now actually sitting in the very house in which my father had been brought up. If only I had had a better reason for being here.

We looked over as the door opened, and watched the trolley being wheeled in and come to rest between us.

"This is Anne," she said, introducing the elderly lady. "Anne, this is John. Anne's in charge of the house," she told me. "John's my great nephew," she said to her.

I sat sipping my tea, listening intently to her descriptions of my grandparents, and other close relatives most whom I had never heard of. I had no intention of asking her for the money, not right now. I didn't want anything to change between us, to spoil the feeling that I had of once more being part of my father's family.

Later, as I made my way down the driveway, having promised to return with the fire extinguisher, I knew that asking her for the money on my next visit, wasn't going to be any easier. She was no longer a distant family figure, but an old lady I liked and was glad to be related to. I wanted her to like me in return and who, apart from a disreputable moneylender, would think much of someone asking them for a loan, to repay a loan.

---

chapter
eleven

'WHAT WAS I DOING HERE', I ASKED MYSELF, sitting outside these shops again? Shops were places you went into to buy something, not to sell something, especially not a fire extinguisher, and not on an afternoon like this, with the rain pouring down and the prospect of losing your job hanging over your head.

As a boy, I had never known what I wanted to be when I grew up but now, somewhat later on in life, I at least knew what I definitely did not want to be, and this was it.

I didn't feel like a salesman. I felt more like an actor in a long-running play. I knew my lines backward but I would still have to work flat out to give them a convincing ring.

But what else could I do? Another period of unemployment, this time without any savings to cushion my fall, would be really and truly the end of the line.

It was the first time I had ever felt quite so bad. I had nothing left to give. I couldn't bring myself to get out of the car. What was the point? These shopkeepers weren't going to be any different from the ones I had visited yesterday.

I sat for a while nursing my despair, but not yet feeling I was beyond the reach of that self-help I had so often fallen back on in the past. Somewhere in the Book Collection there were bound to be men whose example I could surely follow, men who had had their backs to the wall just like me.

But which ones? I had to be careful in making a choice like this if I wasn't to be merely some crackpot trying to turn his dreams into reality.

It was an event rather than a personality that first came to mind. Wasn't my situation a bit like the one the Germans were in during their attack on Russia in the Second World War? Even if I did make a sale and win a tactical victory, worthy of the many achieved early on by the Germans in Operation Barbarossa, what good would it do? They had grossly underestimated the vast distances they had had to cover and the strength of their opponent. My offensive, like theirs, would probably grind to a halt. Tomorrow, there would be the same reluctance to get out of the car, the same likelihood that the sale might not come until I had reached the last shop, that it might not come at all.

But what about the actual people, rather than the events, in the Book Collection? What had they done when they were in a situation like this? I thought of Hitler staring at a painting of Frederick the Great, while the Russian tanks approached his Bunker. I thought of Churchill thinking of his distant relative, the famous Duke of Marlborough. But I had to do better than this, for the only picture I had ever stared at for any length of time was the one on the Sales Office wall, and a shallow river with ducks on it would hardly provide me with the inspiration I needed.

It looked for a while as if the Book Collection was going to let me down and it was all I had, at that point, to keep me from sinking into the abyss. My flask was empty, and my legs were getting into a cramp, when at last the idea came to me.

I thought again of that great battlefield in Russia where the German armies in Operation Barbarossa had made their initial advance, just like I had done as I had travelled down that row of shops. Like me they had covered a lot of ground but, also like me, they had been swallowed up by the enormity of their task. Surely, they had been sorely in need of a change of plan?

Which was what I needed, too, I realised, and I wasn't going to leave it too late, like they had. To get me properly started, therefore, I took a leaf out of another book. Sent to help the French stop Hitler in the same World War, Lord Gort the Commander in Chief of the British Expeditionary Force had gone against his orders and the defeatist flow and moved two divisions over to the left of the battlefield in time to save his army, and almost certainly his country too, from defeat.

Directing my energies at shopkeepers, I could see now, was wrong. I was learning from history, I thought excitedly. The maximum effort cold calling required would at the best bring only minimal results, a series of mere tactical victories. What I needed wasn't just a change of direction, it was a completely new strategy.

*

I lifted the Directory from the shelf and laid it before me on the desk. If I could make telephone contact with the right people in some of these big companies then maybe I could turn the whole thing around.

I knew I would have to put all I had into this and enthused by my mood swing I began to devise my plan of campaign. It didn't matter if I was in danger of letting my imagination run away with me, it was the result that counted. I wasn't having delusions of grandeur either. I knew I wasn't as imposing as Hitler or Churchill. But I felt confident that even someone of lesser stamp, like myself, would be able to carry out what I now had in mind.

Ready for action I dialled the first number in the Directory of Big Companies, deciding to adopt the no-nonsense approach of a lesser-ranked Company Commander.

"Cairns Décor. How can I help you?"

"Could you tell me the name of the person in your company who is responsible for Fire Protection? I asked.

"Fire Protection?"

"Yes, extinguishers etc," I explained, in the confident tone of someone to be reckoned with.

"John Summers," she said, not cutting me off, but instantly telling me what I wanted to know, signifying that I had achieved what had been my first, clearly-defined objective. I had identified my target. Nothing much, it would seem, but I knew better.

"Thank you very much for your help, I stated, replacing the receiver.

Tight-lipped and more in control of myself than I had been for a long time I sat for a while contemplating the success of my imaginative approach. As I was about to move to the next stage I saw a way whereby the operation I was conducting might be given an even better chance of success. I felt free to indulge myself yet further.

Taking command of a submarine I saw the Directory as my chart, whilst the telephone, by transforming sound into sight, became my periscope.

I knew Admiral Doenitz, in the Book Collection, had required his U Boats to carry out in training sixty-six surface and sixty-six submerged attacks, before they even fired their first torpedo. But I also knew I would have to manage without all this, and anyway, he had been on the losing side.

"John Summers please," I asked, having dialled the same number again after a suitable period of time had elapsed. By asking for 'John' on this occasion rather than 'Mister', she would be likely to think I knew the man, raise the boom, and put me through. A sound tactic. That is, if I really did know better.

"John Summers," said a voice. It had worked. I had got through.

"Hello, Mr Summers. John Grant from Barton Fire Protection here."

"Who?"

The voice was that of a middle-aged man, his tone suggesting, as I hoped mine did too, that he was someone to be reckoned with. Contact had been made.

"Barton Fire, Mr Summers. Could you possibly tell me when you usually review your contract for the annual servicing of your fire extinguishers" I asked, so that I could set my sights.

"Next month, actually."

"Would it be possible for us to get the opportunity of quoting for the work? We should be able to make savings for you," I said to him, feeling a little bit as if I was pleading for my life. And 'savings' – one of the best weapons I had on board.

"We're always looking for savings," came the welcome reply.

"Could I drop in sometime in the near future and have a quick look at your equipment? Before I make up the quote, I mean," I pleaded yet further.

"You can indeed," I heard, feeling that I had just scored a hit.

But I would still have to be careful, I knew. 'Dropping in' to see him didn't mean I had sunk anything. He could still stay afloat by not being there in person when I called, leaving me with no more than the opportunity of sending in a written quote. This would be miles off target. I would have to pin him down.

"If I call in to see you on Monday, would that be okay?"

"Next Monday …?"

"Any day next week Mr Summers."

"Monday should be all right. Say about two."

"Two's fine. I look forward to meeting you, Mr Summers, and thank you very much for your courtesy. I'll send you a short letter, with some Company literature, etc." I told him in heartfelt relief at my success and in a tone of voice filled with gratitude.

"Excellent," came the final confirmation.

Having repeated the process with all twenty of the companies on the first page of the directory, I felt pleased with the three direct hits I'd scored. I lowered the periscope and decided to let the submarine sail itself for a while, as I assessed the overall effects of the operation.

Although I hadn't sold anything yet, an appointment with the right person at the right time was a long way down the road to success. The commission I might have earned from cold calling on shops, if I had been able to sustain the effort, was nothing to what I could make from these big companies, with their often several hundred extinguishers needing serviced and replaced throughout the year. If I could pull this off then my whole situation was bound to take a turn for the better.

My optimism, and the self-confidence it gave rise to, were soon bolstered by yet another passage from the Book Collection. There were three kinds of officer, I had read, those who were industrious and stupid, who should be got rid of; those who were clever and industrious, who were suitable for the top staff jobs; and those who were clever and lazy, ideally suited for the very top jobs of all.

It was a great pity, I felt, that Sears, who should be got rid of, was in the first group while I myself, suitable for the very top job, was officially at the bottom.

I really needed these sales appointments. Cold calling on shops wasn't an option. If I couldn't break into these big companies then there was no way I was going to avoid the huge financial iceberg that lay directly in my path.

I maybe had more in common with the submariner than I thought. I had to get it right. I had to do a good job. For both of us, the consequences of failure would be disastrous. But I wasn't going to fail, lose my house, lose my job. I was going to be a salesman, a real salesman.

chapter
twelve

IF A HOUSE THAT HAD BEEN LIVED IN FOR MANY years could almost be thought to have a personality, endearing itself to its owners, could such a house also communicate in some way with subsequent generations, who had never lived in it. As I followed Bethea into a room on the other side of the hallway I saw that the fireplace was huge, made of wood and marble, and that there was extensive wooden panelling on the walls. These weren't things that I was used to and yet I felt at home, not like someone who had come to borrow money or to deliver a fire extinguisher at cost price.

"And how long has this house been in the family?" I asked, looking about me but trying not to stare at things as if I was at an exhibition. "My mother once told me about it," I added.

"It belonged to your great great grandfather, actually. To my grandfather."

"As far back as that?" I gasped.

"Your mother was a fine woman," she then said, taking up my mention of her. "I suppose you would get the books."

"You mean the Collection. I certainly did," I told her, assuming that she meant the contents of the boxes I had found in the attic and feeling surprised that she knew about them.

"And are you a reader, too?" she asked.

"Yes."

"You've got readers on both sides of your family, so that's not a surprise," she told me, with an approving nod. "And do you paint or anything?"

"Paint? You mean like an artist? No, I'm afraid not," I stated, wondering why she had asked, and feeling that I had just owned up to something.

"You don't. You're just a reader. Well a lot of these books originally belonged to your father," she informed me, as if revealing a secret. "The classics, like Dickens, and the Short Story collections, would be your mother's all right, but the heavier ones, history, etc., they would be your father's."

"So my father was a reader too, was he?"

"A great reader, even more than your mother," she affirmed.

"So that's who I take it off," I replied, pleased that one of my two lone indulgences now carried a genetic stamp of approval.

"And how is your Aunt Grace?" she asked, as if she had read my thoughts. Grace only read the Bible, I certainly hadn't taken after her.

"Fine. Well, she's in residential care. But fine."

"I suppose she'll have filled you in on all the gory details about us," she continued, with a knowing smile.

"No. Not really," I lied.

"I suppose she's still religious."

I wasn't happy with this definition. It was 'religious' people who had crucified Christ, according to the Pastor, and Grace certainly wasn't a hypocrite, or a moral snob, or anything like that. Grace was the real thing, not perfect, but sincere in her beliefs and in her actions too.

"Yes," I replied. "Still a great churchgoer, when she can manage."

"And you?" Bethea asked.

"Well, in a way," I said hesitantly, anxious to avoid the complexity of an honest answer.

"There's something I have to get from Anne," she said, unexpectedly getting to her feet, and leaving me to continue alone with my thoughts.

If I was 'in a way' getting to be a bit like Grace in my beliefs then I certainly didn't go the whole way with her, although the fact that 'God was still on the throne', as she put it, and wreaked vengeance on the nations by way of famines, floods and pestilence had at various times made me sit up and think. Tsunamis, famines and epidemics, in the news every other day, certainly lent strength to her argument even if they didn't prove anything. But I had never allowed things like this to affect me too much and her warning about their relevance to my 'unregenerate' state had been something I was able to live with. What the Pastor had to say on this subject was proving to be a bit more challenging. But that was another matter.

Aunt Grace's concern for my spiritual welfare went back as far as I could remember, coming to the boil now and again, as on one occasion when my large bony hands had been drawn to her attention by my piano teacher and given as a reason for my lack of progress. Bony hands just like these, apparently, and the pair of strong shoulders that I had too, were once possessed by her uncle who, unruly as a boy, had gone on to become an equally unruly boxer, both inside and outside the ring.

I had uncertain feelings about facts like this. Was I to feel ashamed, like Grace, that my great great uncle had been inclined to fight outside the ring, as well as in it, or proud that I could, like him, deliver a very heavy punch when I had to. I preferred the latter, for my large bony hands, more suited to delivering blows than they were to playing the piano, had proved quite useful from time to time.

But, apart from the fact that this had put me in the top ten in playground brawls, and in the bottom ten of those likely to be bullied, I felt her fears, that I might be in possession of a rogue gene, were groundless. I was quite good-natured, much more than I was quite good at fighting, and quite good at avoiding challenges rather than facing up to them. Surely my love of Chopin, usually played on CD by somebody else of course, and my compulsion to read history books, made it unlikely I would follow in the boxer's footsteps, inside or outside the ring.

"A strong-minded woman, your Aunt Grace," Bethea pronounced, as she came back into the room, carrying a parcel of some sort. "Nothing like your mother. But then close relatives often aren't like each other, are they? I'm nothing like my father, your great grandfather, or your father for that matter. Couldn't paint to save my life."

"Paint?"

"In oils mainly. But in water-colours too, of course."

"My father was an artist?"

"Oh yes, didn't you know?"

"I'd heard he was good at drawing."

"He certainly was. Took it off my father. Your father didn't make money at it, or anything like that, but he definitely had some of the talent. Do you have any interest in the subject?"

"Well, there's a picture I look at," I began, "but I couldn't even draw a bottle in the art class at school," I told her, taking refuge in a forthright reply.

"Never mind. A gift is a gift. You don't earn it, and it's not your fault if you don't have it. But you should know about your great grandfather," she added. "I'm surprised that no one has ever told you."

"Really good, was he?"

"Gold medal at the Paris Salon – when he was 28, and again when he was 48. I'll say he was good," she said with enthusiasm. "So that's something for you to be proud of. I suppose you've only heard the bad things about this side of your family."

I wished she hadn't come back to this again. I felt a little ashamed now, at my willingness to believe that my father's family weren't up to much. That my Aunt Grace had disapproved of them, and that I had gone along with her for so long, didn't say much for me, or for that matter, the human race in general. But this is what people did, allowing important matters to lie unaddressed because of the opinions of others and because doing nothing was so easy.

And it wasn't just people who did this. Whole nations had done it too. Wasn't that what America had done in her isolationist policy towards Europe before World War II? According to the Book Collection, in her anxiety to avoid war American Isolationism had helped nourish conditions abroad in which her own ultimate safety could only be secured by the greatest war effort in her history. She certainly wasn't subscribing to it now, and Britain wasn't either. But a lot of people seemed to have missed the point. And I had, too, up to now, but what had the cost been to me of adopting such an attitude?

'Let them be. You're better off without them', was what my Aunt Grace had said about my father's side of the family. For years I had obeyed this injunction without ever challenging it. Her point of view had had that down-to-earth ring about it, the kind that appealed to the hard-hearted, to moral cowards, to gullible people, and of course to lazy people, such as myself.

That Aunt Grace could have been wrong, of course sincerely wrong, about all this was something that at long last was beginning to dawn on me.

"I've not heard only bad things, exactly" I finally answered, evasively.

"But not exactly good ones either?"

"I suppose not," I said slowly, hovering on the brink of a confrontation that I wished to avoid. Having at last got in touch with her, after suppressing my interest for so long, I wasn't going to throw it all away on an impulsive need to say something, especially since I had begun to call my Aunt Grace's attitude towards her into question. Bethea had come into possession of my great grandfather's money because she had been the oldest child, and the only one who had reached adulthood when he died. I had always known this but I could see it differently now. This didn't make me a victim, as Grace would have it, I was more like a casualty.

Grace was wrong to say that my father's share of my grandfather's money should have come to me for, in the strictly legal sense, he had never had a share. He had however had various amounts of money over the years as a helping hand from Bethea and for all anyone knew it could have added up to quite a lot. He had certainly had had an inheritance of some sort.

To say that Bethea had withheld money from my mother after my father's early death didn't hold up either. Exactly what money had she been due? My father hadn't, strictly speaking, inherited anything that should have been passed on to her. And even Grace had admitted that Bethea had offered some kind of help, so she couldn't have been all that bad.

"I don't suppose Grace told you about the Food Importers." Bethea said to me in a challenging tone of voice.

"I didn't think you even knew I worked in a Food Importers," I exclaimed.

"Never knew?" she protested. "How do you think you got there in the first place?"

"Sorry," I replied, genuinely puzzled.

"The present owner's family were friends of ours. Didn't you know that, either?"

"I don't remember anyone ever mentioning it."

"If it hadn't been for your Aunt Grace's attitude we could have done a lot more for you in that place too. And I don't expect she told you that we paid your school fees?"

"I suppose I'd be too young," I answered, taken aback, unable to think of anything meaningful to say.

If the main purpose of my visit had been to ask for money, then where I fitted into my father's family now seemed much more important. They hadn't forgotten about me, after all, and now that I thought about it, how could my Aunt Grace have afforded my school fees, anyway? And hadn't there been a mantle of protection over me at the Food Importers, before the old boss, a son of the founder, had retired? The other side of my family didn't belong to the other side, after all. But where would I belong if I asked Bethea for money? I couldn't do it now.

"I've brought you the extinguisher. It's in the car," I told her cheerfully.

When I returned, the tea trolley had appeared and, as she filled the cups, I took the extinguisher from its carton and displayed it on my lap.

"I've got something for you, too," she said, reaching for the parcel that lay propped up against the side of the trolley. But first, take your tea and as many cakes and buns as you like."

I guessed from the shape of the object outlined within the thick brown paper in which it was wrapped that the parcel contained a picture. But would it be a print or an original? A print would be all right, but an original could be something much more than that.

It would hardly be a print, I concluded, my spirits soaring. Surely Bethea would only have originals since the artist had been her father. That he had won the Gold Medal at the Paris Salon when everybody knew that so many now world famous artists had almost been thrown out of the place surely meant the picture would be worth something. Things were beginning to look up.

chapter
thirteen

"So you do fire extinguishers," the man said, as he greeted me in the foyer. "I'm the MD in here. Shall we discuss things in the my office."

He looked capable and energetic, and I hoped I looked as good to him. This was more than just a sales appointment, it was where I was going to meet with success or failure in my final attempt to get on top of the job.

Following him down a long corridor, I spotted a Fire Exit sign which lacked the required illustration of a running man on it and, better still, I saw through an open door a computer room, on the wall of which hung a Dry Powder extinguisher, whose emissions, I knew, could damage the equipment as much as a fire could. Those were technical titbits I could keep up my sleeve for later use, I muttered to myself.

"Thank you for seeing me, Mr Summers," I began, as I settled in front of the desk of this well-dressed, middle-aged man who, although he didn't look like he posed a threat, nevertheless had the power to dash my hopes, to foil my plans, to turn me into a failure, although that wasn't going to happen, I told myself.

"Is this how you people usually get business? You know, by phoning people?" he asked informally, sounding genuinely interested.

"Quite often, Mr Summers, but we do a lot of advertising in the big directories, too," I informed him, in an authoritative tone of voice.

"Well, what can you do for me?" he asked pleasantly, sitting back in his chair and folding his arms across his chest.

This sounded like a good start, although I knew that it wasn't. He had wrong-footed me with a question, the specific answer to which I didn't know. How could I? I had assured him on the phone that I could deal with all of his fire protection requirements, without knowing what they were. I had brought this on myself therefore. That it was the name of the game, and that there was only so much you could say in an initial telephone call like that, didn't excuse the lapse. I should have found out more.

"We can supply you with all the equipment you are likely to need, Mr Summers," I told him, "and we can provide you with a very high level of service, too."

I had done it again. Another pitiful generality. I very quickly had to do better, I told myself anxiously.

"And how do you know exactly what I need?" he asked, the expression on his face indicating neither approval nor disapproval of my dismal overture. Maybe I was being too hard on myself.

But my sales prospect was certainly doing much better than I was. He should have been the salesman, not me. His questions had been the right ones, from his point of view, and my answers had been the wrong ones, from my point of view. I was steering the conversation into oblivion. I had to say something meaningful, and with my very next breath.

"Fire Protection is a bit of a racket," I said, overdoing it and realising almost at once that my remark might sound as if I was making a confession.

"It is?" he asked, looking at me intently as if expecting a further revelation, just as I had feared.

"But not with us," I added hastily. "With Bartons, you can be sure of getting a fair deal."

"That's good to know."

"Much of the work that is done in Fire Protection is unnecessary," I told him, deciding to stick with this controversial idea. After all, I wasn't a surgeon or a concert pianist. A blatant mistake was maybe something I could turn to my advantage.

"With us you'll get a fair deal, Mr Summers. I can assure you of that. We don't just want you to be a customer, we want you to stay a customer," I told him, falling back on the words I was inclined to use with the shopkeepers. "And we know you won't stay with us unless you're absolutely sure we're doing a good job, at the right price, and that we can be trusted," I added breathlessly, hoping this would move things to the next stage.

"And how many extinguishers do you have?" I asked him, almost panting, persuading myself that things might, in spite of the bad start, be going according to plan. But wasn't that what Field Marshal Haig, Commander in Chief of the British Expeditionary Force, had often claimed in the First World War when his armies were being decimated? On the other hand, Field Marshal Montgomery in the Second World War had often been accused of doing something similar although he, unlike Haig, had usually won the battle. I tried to remain optimistic. Hadn't both these men, in the end, been recipients of the victor's crown.

"I have, say, about five hundred extinguishers, he replied hesitantly. "And we have quite a few fire hoses, too. A delicate operation."

This was the kind of thing I had been hoping for – a possible way ahead. Not his hesitancy over the number of extinguishers. But delicate? A delicate operation!

We specialise in Health and Safety matters," I pronounced, in the sombre tone of voice I felt appropriate to this more elevated aspect of the work.

"I'm interested in that."

"It's the main feature of our service," I said, exaggerating, feeling I was making progress at last. "We employ a man especially for it."

"Interesting."

I believed him. I was definitely on the right lines.

"He'd be at your service in an advisory capacity," I added.

"Look ... eh, John. If you can do a quick calculation on what you would charge for doing these servicing operations," he said, handing me a typewritten list, "maybe we can take things a bit further."

As I looked down at the paper, he handed me a second sheet which I saw was an invoice from his current supplier of fire equipment. It was a gift, showing me the prices I would have to beat. He was making it easy for me.

I could see it all quite clearly now, almost as if it had come straight out of the Sale Manual. I had identified his need. There was a lot of paint in this place and a lot of paint could mean a big fire, and a big fire could mean a lot of insurance. This man had to have just the right models in just the right place. They had to be very well maintained. And he had to have written evidence of it. He had to have the right safety signs, too. And he had to be able to extinguish a fire, as soon as it started, with the very best of equipment. That I should have realised all this before was academic. I had found out in time. If anything went wrong in this place then my sales prospect would take the fall. This was it. He had to cover his back.

And he had come to the right person. Or, rather, the right person had come to him. I had opened up this sales opportunity, and I was going to close it.

"We can more or less take the sting out of all these things Mr Summers," I told him reassuringly.

I could ease his anxiety about health and safety, about insurance and fire protection in general, and I could help him look good about it. Price wasn't the main issue, this was.

"I'll get our man to come in and do a survey for you. That's if you decide to go with us, of course, and he'll point out anything needing put right. He'll do it all for you, absolutely everything, with all the necessary paperwork submitted to you for your approval, of course."

"Sounds good," came the words I wanted to hear.

"As for price," I continued in a casual tone as I saw his gaze fall questioningly on the invoice. "If I can reduce your annual bill by a nominal sum, say 5%, and still provide these extra services would that sound all right?"

"It would and …"

"You'll be fully compliant with all the recent fire regulations. We'll take the whole thing off your hands completely," I repeated yet again. "We will, of course, make sure you are in complete control."

"Look John," the Managing Director said, getting up from his desk to where I was seated holding the invoice. "I'm having hassle with all these Health and Safety Regulations, and the fire extinguisher people we're using aren't up to the job. Our warehouses are packed with inflammables, and the insurance people aren't happy with our present arrangements."

I'm not in the least bit surprised," I said in a sympathetic tone, pleased that the faith I had placed in my intuitive perception had been vindicated and, additionally, that I had been given the opportunity to deliver my technical titbits with what I felt to be an artistic flourish. "I noticed a dry powder extinguisher in the computer room," I told him. "If you ever have to use it, it'll ruin every computer it touches. The correct fire extinguisher for that kind of fire risk is a CO2 – the discharge will evaporate," I stated.

"I wouldn't have a clue about that" he said with deference.

"And the Fire Exit sign, halfway down the corridor, is non compliant with British Standards, too. It doesn't have an illustration of a running man on it. It's almost worse than having no sign at all," I said, feeling good that I had managed to work my wavering efforts up into such a satisfactory climax.

"Is that right?" he stated, in an even more deferential tone of voice, as he ran his hand down the prices on the invoice.

"And you can reduce these prices?" he asked. "By 5%?"

"Certainly," I announced, looking him firmly in the eye.

"And you can sort this fire protection mess out for me while I'm busy trying to be the Managing Director of this place?" he asked, delighting me with the intimacy of his words.

"I can, Mr Summers," I stated solemnly.

I watched feverishly as he walked back round his desk at which he sat for a moment, looking down, avoiding my eyes.

I would be landing this contract by what I felt was a very slick piece of salesmanship, I told myself, still a little shakily, since he hadn't signed anything. Not knowing at first what his requirements actually were, I had ridden this out, kept a clear head, and as soon as I had sensed his real need, had brought maximum force to bear on it. I had been a staff officer on the phone and a company commander in the field, all rolled into one. This had been a maximum effort. I had pulled it off. I had what it takes.

"I like what you have to offer, John," he said, at last looking up, with his pen in his hand.

"When we come to renew the contract in a few weeks time, your offers will be one of the very first we will look at."

I felt what remained of my nervous energy drain away. How could I recover from this?, I asked myself. After all my efforts, I had failed to actually close the sale. My intuitive perception hadn't been enough and my technical titbits and all my posturing had been in vain. I couldn't, like Haig, call the disaster a mere set-back or, like Montgomery, skilfully bring maximum force to bear somewhere else. I didn't feel I had enough strength left in me to do either of these.

This was probably how Ribbentrop, Hitler's Foreign Minister, had felt the day after the signing of the Pact with Moscow in 1939, which had removed the immediate Russian threat and given Hitler a freer hand elsewhere. Up until then, according to the details described in that particular book, everything had seemed to be working out exactly as Ribbentrop had planned, even better. Like me, how he must have soared in his own self esteem. His "boss" was delighted. But, contrary to what he had hoped would follow, Britain had kept her guarantee to Poland and the alliance with Italy hadn't materialised. And I, after all my efforts and my optimism, hadn't secured the contract with Cairns Décor, or sold even one fire extinguisher.

What I read had taken two days to transpire in Ribbentrop's case had taken only minutes in mine, but my failure had been enough to send me into the same precarious situation that he had been in as he realised there was nothing he could do about the terrible events about to take place. His "boss" hadn't been pleased either, to say the least. I would have that in common with him, too.

The idea of confronting another sales prospect only to end up in the same position as I was in now, filled me with horror and like Ribbentrop, I couldn't just walk away. I had to face the consequences. What eventually befell him, he was hanged as a war criminal in 1946, was something I didn't want to dwell on for what had just happened was bad, very bad, and my future looked almost, if not quite, as bleak as his had turned out to be.

chapter fourteen

AS I DROVE INTO THE ESTATE, DEPRESSED, brooding on my failure to close the sale, my spirits rose slightly as I thought of the painting lying on the back seat. I wondered how much it would fetch.

I unwrapped it, as soon as I got in, and laid it on my lap. My great grandfather's name, clearly written on the bottom right-hand corner, was something I felt good about, regardless of its crucial monetary value. But at the same time I was looking for something quite different from either of these things.

There was a smudginess about the faces of the two girls in the scene but it didn't look so bad when I sat the painting on a chair across the room from me. From this distance the girls, and the sea in which they were splashing, came to life.

Could this picture be made to serve some useful purpose, like the one in the Sales Office? I asked myself. That scene on the riverbank had, at the very least, provided me with a framework on which to support my daydreams and had often taken the edge off the hopelessness of my surroundings. What could this one do for me?

Although I liked the sea, and I liked children, I couldn't say that the picture made me want to join in their frolics. It certainly wasn't a scene that inspired me or drew me into it. It wasn't a picture that I would have chosen for myself, I had to conclude. But since I was thinking of selling it, not buying it, I knew the important question really was, how much would I get for it?

*

"It's a John Grant, all right," the art dealer announced, lifting the picture up to within a few inches of his nose.

"Have you had it for long?" he asked.

"Not long," I told him. "I'm related to the artist," I added hastily, to strengthen my image in these unfamiliar surroundings.

"And you are exactly …?"

"His great grandson."

"How interesting. And do you have any more of his paintings?"

"Only this one, I'm afraid."

"Well, it's not one of your great grandfather's better known paintings, Mr Grant," he declared, "but I expect you will already know that."

"I'm a bit out of touch," I lied.

That the painting was genuine was not what I had come to find out. I already knew that. Nor did I really care if it had artistic merit, at least I thought at first I didn't. but I could ask him if it had, at least for a start, before I got round to the more important question.

"And where does he fit into things nowadays?" I asked, as if I had some background knowledge of the art world.

"Well, he was influenced by McTaggart, and by the Dutch School with regard to the figures …," the dealer began.

"But he's still quite well thought of?" I asked, politely but anxiously.

"Oh yes. Absolutely."

Laying the painting on an easel standing beside his desk, the dealer settled back in his chair, staring appreciatively at my great grandfather's creation.

How different this was from sitting across the desk from Sears, I thought. Here, I was being treated with respect, as an owner of an oil painting, as a whole person. Sitting across the desk from people like Sears, the psychological advantage such people always had adding weight to their empty words and forcing you to agree with them, had been a humiliating experience. It looked like things were about to improve at last. This picture might be valuable enough to take some of the financial pressure off me, surely, I calculated.

"It's not one of his better known paintings," the dealer pronounced again, "but thanks for bringing it in, Mr Grant. It would be passed down to you?" he asked, raising his eyebrows.

"From my Great Aunt."

"And does she have any others?"

"Oh yes," I said, guessing that Bethea would have quite a few of what to her would be almost like family photographs.

"Well I'd be delighted to have a look at them. Works from his later period can fetch a very good price. Your Great Grandfather is becoming very popular with the collectors, I must say."

"I'll certainly mention it to her," I said casually, basking in my status as a near relative of someone important.

I lifted the painting from the easel and studied it. "It's not exactly my cup of tea," I said in the same tone. "Kind of smudgy." I added.

"That's the influence of Israels," he informed me, making me feel pleased that I had made what must have sounded like a perceptive and highly relevant remark.

"Israels?"

"The great Josef Israels. Grant was influenced by him. An art critic once described this particular aspect of his work, which was different from his usual style, as a crumbly impasto of disagreeable quality."

"The critics don't like him?" I asked, resentful of the fact that someone other than myself might not appreciate the work of my prominent family member.

"Oh no. Quite the contrary," the art dealer said, contradicting me. "The man who wrote that was lambasted by his peers, actually, but it does touch on the 'smudginess', if I may use your word. Most of his paintings don't have this particular quality and are quite beautiful."

"Well I think I've taken up enough of your time," I told him, my resentment quickly subsiding. "Thank you very much for being so informative and helpful."

"My pleasure, Mr Grant. I hope you will indeed mention me to your Great Aunt, and that I might hear from her."

I wrapped the painting in its bubbled plastic wrapping and slipped it into the carrier bag.

"Oh yes. He's becoming a great collector's item," the dealer told me again, negotiating the easel and the desk to accompany me to the door.

My mood changing now, I began to feel like a 'name-dropper' and a fraud in these surroundings, with the only previous painting in my life hanging on the wall at Bartons. But the crucial question, which should have been put at the beginning rather than at the end of the visit, still had to be asked.

"What do you think it's worth?"

"Oh, somewhere in the high hundreds," the dealer declared. "If it had been from his later period it would have been worth a good deal more, considerably more. And of course, the smudginess doesn't help."

*

The amount the dealer had valued the painting at rang in my ears all the way back to the flat. A few hundred pounds would hardly pay the electricity bill, far less a fraction of the amount I had to find in the very near future.

As I sat in the chair beside the CD cabinet about to enlist the help of Chopin, I realised that, like some under-strength drug, the soothing effect of the music wasn't going to be enough on this occasion. To be without hope was about as bad as it could get.

In my efforts to sell fire extinguishers I had not only stretched my powers of persuasion to the limit but I had also gone against that inner voice which condemned all the inaccuracies and half truths that most salesman so often had to utter.

Even if I had been successful, the financial rewards might still not have been enough to solve my problems anyway, I knew. But I hadn't been successful. I had sold absolutely nothing.

To be without hope was certainly bad but, to have entertained false hopes, as I had been doing with this picture, seemed to be even worse. I had hoped it might fetch a few thousand pounds at least and had ended up with the prospect of only a few hundred.

chapter
fifteen

As I went into the Old Toll Bar Big Tom spotted me and waved across like an old friend. The others were there too.

They certainly might come from a social group that I was unfamiliar with, that I found hard to define, but I no longer felt uneasy in their company. They seemed, for the most part, to be bright and intelligent and they certainly weren't hampered, like I was, by thoughts on their uncertain pathway through life.

"You're invited, John," Big Tom said to me as I took my seat.

"Where to?"

"The caravan park," Andy answered. "You'll enjoy it."

"Come on, John, say you'll come," Liz coaxed. We need a new face up there."

They sat smiling at me expectantly and, without asking for any more information, I agreed to go. Rows of caravans would dull the memory of rows of shops and they would provide a change of scene from girls splashing about in the water, too. Just what I needed.

"You'll like the place. Two six berth vans, and you get a marvellous view of the sea," Karen said encouragingly.

"And the company's really good too," added Liz, rolling her eyes.

"When do we leave?" I asked, beginning to feel quite good about taking a trip like this.

*

As we unloaded our gear at the site, Big Tom carried the girls' bags into their caravan, leaving them free to prepare refreshments.

The park was spacious, situated on high ground overlooking the sea, and a faint sound of music wafted towards us from a communal building we had passed on the way in. The only member of the group not wearing shorts, I was glad of the pair Andy threw across the caravan to me. I could see Liz and Karen at a table outside setting up some glasses and tumblers and Big Tom opening a bottle.

As we went out, Andy switched on his radio and screwed up his face to the strains of 'Land of Hope and Glory', at once flicking the controls to produce a Country and Western sound. Tom dragged Liz towards him and forced her to dance with him round the table. I guessed from the way she was responding, manoeuvring him as she had done with me at the party that, if there was anything between them, he was going to have an easier task ahead of him with Liz than I was going to have with Linda. But I liked both of them a lot and felt good about the idea of them getting together.

I joined Andy and Karen, clapping in rhythm with the melody and shouting words of encouragement, while just beyond them, in contrast, lay the open sea, motionless and silent.

Later, we all made our way down to the beach to throw pebbles and paddle our feet.

This break wouldn't solve anything, I thought forlornly, but my thoughts on selling, or rather on not selling, fire extinguishers began to fade into the back of my mind and with them the memory of my disappointing excursion into the art world.

The next day everyone seemed as content as I was to lounge on their deck chairs and be soothed by Country and Western music. The sun warmed us from a clear blue sky and only a beach ball that occasionally bounced among us, kicked by a group of youngish men playing outside a nearby caravan, disturbed us.

When the ball, this time hitting the table, knocked over an empty glass of lager, some of the dregs splashed onto Liz's blouse and she sat up, startled.

Big Tom rose quickly and trapped the ball at his feet, as he had done a few times before but on this occasion, to my surprise, he didn't kick it back. Instead, he looked enquiringly at Andy.

Staring in the direction from which the ball had come, a hand shielding his eyes from the sun, Andy shook his head peevishly before signalling Big Tom, with a wave of his hand, to return the ball to its owners. As we settled back down on our chairs, the radio continued to emit its Country and Western sounds only to fall silent a few minutes later, as the beach ball knocked it off-station and nearly off the table.

Once again Big Tom rose quickly and trapped the ball at his feet while its owners, the group of youngish men, stood impatiently looking over at us for the ball to be returned.

Big Tom sat back down, placing the ball underneath his deck chair.

"They don't really mean any harm," Karen said to him soothingly.

"They don't?" Andy asked her, a feigned look of innocence on his face.

"What do you think you're f'n playing at?" a sweaty-looking man in vest and shorts shouted as he strode angrily in our direction.

"Who, me?" Tom asked, unconvincingly.

The man, joined now by one of his companions, glanced sideways at Andy, who had sat up and was leaning forward on his deck chair.

"Yes you. Give me the f'n ball," he said to Tom. "And you can keep your face out of it," he said, looking again at Andy.

Andy stood up.

"Don't," Karen said to him, reaching over to grab his arm.

"Don't what?" Andy asked, sounding mildly indignant.

"Just don't," Karen repeated.

"Go on Tom," she gently pleaded, "give them the ball."

Tom remained seated, looking over at Andy.

"Oh give them the bloody thing," Andy told him, glancing meekly at Karen.

"Do the women give the orders here?" the man asked Andy. "Come on, give me the f'n ball," he said again to Tom.

This was not unlike what had happened outside Liz's flat. It was as though Andy and Tom saw what was happening as some kind of game. A game they were familiar with, and were quite keen to play.

"On second thoughts I'm not sure we're going to give you the ball," Andy said, stepping closer to the man who glared at him, a look of disbelief on his face. He moved back as Andy took a further step towards him.

Tom, his size now becoming evident as he got to his feet, had meanwhile moved towards the man's companion and was standing a few paces from him, his hands at first on his hips, then hanging loosely by his sides.

Karen looked over at me, shrugged, and shook her head in resignation. She had realised, as I could see reflected on the faces of the ball's two owners, that Andy and Tom had made up their minds about something.

"We just want the ball," the first man said, in a slightly subdued tone of voice.

"And if we don't give it to you?" Andy asked, in a similar tone.

"We just want the ball," the same man repeated. "We don't want any trouble."

"I don't either. But you're beginning to change our minds," Andy said, looking over to watch Tom take a few steps closer to the man's companion.

Tom's would-be opponent looked well set up, and he looked fit, too. But it was obvious that a change had come over him. He no longer seemed sure about what he was doing there. He was backing away from Tom, and it was easy to see why.

"Look mate, I'm sorry we got off to a bad start with you," the other man said to Andy. "The heat's going for us."

"And the ball?" Andy asked him.

"It won't come near you again."

"Well, if you're sure," Andy said, his face expressionless.

"I'm sorry about all this," the main said, in a polite tone of voice, glancing at Karen.

"Oh give him the bloody thing," Andy said to Tom.

*

As we settled back down on our deck chairs, the threat caused by the ball removed and the radio back on station, I saw again that Andy had to be more than a fire extinguisher salesman.

As I had watched him stand facing that man, although he wasn't much taller than I was myself, or much broader when he was wearing a suit, he had seemed perfectly at home with the idea of having to resort to violence. He had shown no trace of nerves and had looked capable of moving quickly and becoming a serious obstacle if he got in anyone's way. The man and his companion had obviously seen this too. And then there was Big Tom, which said it all. Andy definitely wasn't a stranger to this kind of thing, and Big Tom seemed to be in his element.

"Anyone fancy a swim?" Liz asked, after a while.

"I do," said Karen, getting up and stretching herself in delightful silhouette against the sun.

"Anyone else?"

"Big Tom stood up too.

Watching them go, Andy and I settled back down on our deck chairs.

Woman was made for man, I reflected philosophically, feeling sorry the girls had gone. But man was made for man, too, in an entirely different but equally important way, I felt, as I watched Andy refill our glasses. It was good to have a friend like him, someone you felt outclassed you in some way, who could do things you couldn't do. Someone whose background and personality were so very different from yours and yet whose spirit nevertheless seemed similar in some essential way to your own. I was glad I had met someone like him.

"Oh yes, Cairns Décor, the big paint company," I told him, in answer to his question. Although I was surprised that he had asked me, I guessed he would have a reason for bringing up something like this, the kind of thing we had come here to forget about.

"He's considering my quote. I suppose it's better than nothing."

"Mm," he said, sitting up to face me.

I knew what he was going to say.

"If you can't close it, forget it. Move on to the next one," he said.

"You don't think it's likely I'll get the contract?"

"You're too honest, John, and you project your outlook in life onto other people. With big contracts you've got to try and lower the odds a bit."

"Lower the odds?"

"Offer an inducement. It's too late for that now, and an MD is a bit too high up, but what about some of these other appointments? Fire protection is often handled by ordinary members of staff who don't think their boss pays them enough."

As I sat listening intently to his explanation of how these things were done, I saw again just how different his way of looking at things, his world was, from mine. And yet it was events in my world that had put me under. I was down, and I couldn't get back up. In what way, therefore was my world any better than his?

Andy worked to a different set of values from the ones I was used to, but they seemed to be getting better results. Was I missing something? was the question I was now asking myself about my outlook in life in general.

"Forget the appointments," John," Andy said, with perfect timing. "I've got something more definite for you."

Rising quickly from his chair and going into the caravan, he returned, unfurling a sheet of paper as he did so, which he spread out before us on the table.

"See this?" he said, pointing to a thick black line drawn across the top half of the sheet. "This is the canal."

"What canal?"

"I'll give you a map later," he explained. "This is the canal," he repeated, running his fingers along the line. "And this is the pathway between the canal bank and a small housing estate," he went on, pointing to a slightly thinner black line drawn perpendicular to the first one. "The point is, if you walk up this pathway you can easily check that no one is on it but you, and no one can see you unless they are. When it's clear, which it usually is, you make the drop."

Pressing his forefinger onto a cross clearly marked on one side of the perpendicular black line, he glanced at me with a look of authority on his face. "You'll see a chalk mark on one of the trees, one that has a hollow at the bottom of the trunk. Put the package inside. And that's it. OK."

"Sounds straightforward."

"It is. You'll be on your own, of course, there and back, and there's to be positively no mobiles."

"What if I need to get in touch with you?"

"You don't. Mobiles can cause more problems than they solve in this kind of thing."

"Even if the car breaks down."

"Even that. Join the AA or something. Just do what you would normally do. Keep it simple and clean. And, of course, you'll get a hefty cash payment as soon as you get back."

I felt as if I had just been briefed by a company commander out of the Book Collection. And the spoils of war, a hefty amount, were just what I needed, to put it mildly.

*

That evening, while Andy was away on a short trip and Tom and Liz had gone into the nearby town, I wandered with Karen up to the hall at the far end of the Caravan Park. We stood for a while listening to the music. There was a sense in which Andy had left her in my care, I persuaded myself, and I would be failing in my duty if I didn't ask her to dance.

I had seldom had a partner quite like her. I wondered what she would be thinking of me. Would I seem to be just the right height and just the right build, too? It wasn't likely. But whether or not I would stand a chance with her was academic. It had to be, of course, because of her relationship with Andy.

Not too good at ballroom dancing, when she was dancing with me that is, she tripped over my feet a few times at first. Of course it made no difference to the effect she was having on me. How she looked was of much more consequence to me than how she could dance.

It was the same off the floor, too. As we sat sipping our drinks, watching the other dancers, we hardly spoke and yet she was commanding my full attention. I had said more to a stranger sitting next to me in the Reading Room of the public library. And yet it wasn't an awkward silence, I hoped. She seemed as content as I was.

But I couldn't let this go on for too long. Being with someone like her demanded something of me but again, in view of her relationship with Andy, I felt that there wasn't much more I could do. But I couldn't blame myself for being attracted to her, I told myself guiltily. Who wouldn't be attracted to her? If I hadn't been there, someone else would have been asking her to dance. It was the same as it had been with Liz at the party – girls who looked like they did would attract plenty of attention. It wasn't my fault she looked like this.

On a positive note, however, I felt I had come a long way in my relationship with her. Only a few days ago, in the Old Toll Bar, she had misunderstood me and would hardly speak to me. Although she wasn't saying much now either, it was definitely a different kind of silence. I couldn't expect her to feel about me the way I felt about her but I was sure I had gone up in her estimation. I would have to make do with this in the circumstances. We were getting along fine, and feeling that her presence demanded something of me, was probably just nerves, I told myself, not liking the sound of the word 'excitement.'

I asked her to dance again and only on one occasion, when our eyes met on our way round the floor, did I feel the existence of something between us which I couldn't put into words but which I felt good about. Maybe if we had met in other circumstances things would have been different.

Later, as we strolled back to the caravan, the cool night air inducing a change of mood, I felt like someone who had rented or borrowed an expensive new car, pleased with the fact that people would think she belonged to me. I regretted the darkness and the absence of passers-by.

Growing restless waiting on the others to return, we went down to the beach. In the water, almost up to our knees, we splashed about, aimlessly at first, then with purposeful movements at each other. She stumbled and fell in the water.

As I helped her to her feet, my arm around her waist, I didn't expect her to look at me the way that she did. She didn't seem to be annoyed or embarrassed. She seemed to be enjoying herself, in the same way that I was. Maybe in other circumstances…

chapter
sixteen

It was part of the arrangement I had made with Andy that I wouldn't be told what was actually in the package and I knew that thinking about what it was would do more harm than good. I had agreed to deliver it, whatever its contents were, and I tried to put the question out of my mind.

Most of the cars that appeared behind me seemed to be following me, although I knew that they weren't. One car, however, a blue Mondeo with two men in it, had been in my rear view mirror for far longer than any of the others and, as a precaution, I drew into a lay-by.

As the car approached I peered at a road map, not taking my eyes off its colourful contents until the vehicle had gone well past. I watched it turn off onto a narrow track which led up to a small cottage standing beside a wooded area on the edge of a field. It was a false alarm, obviously, but I nevertheless felt pleased with my vigilant response.

Later, I turned into the estate and had very soon found the pathway that led up to the canal. My first delivery was going to be easy, I felt. There was no-one in the residents' car park and I could see that none of the windows in the adjacent houses directly overlooked it. Strolling up the pathway I turned every so often to check that no-one was following me.

Soon, the canal embankment came into view and, as I had still not spotted the chalk mark, I began to feel less sure of myself. What if I couldn't find it? Having to take the package back to Andy and tell him that I had got lost was something that filled me with dread. Was I going to fall at the first hurdle? Heaven forbid! Fortunately, just as I was thinking I might have to retrace my steps I saw the mark, and very soon had the package snugly tucked up inside the hollow trunk. Confident again, my nervousness beginning to subside into a mere clammy feeling on my forehead and hands, I made my way back to the car.

Reflecting on what I had just done, I felt good about the smoothness of the procedure. As Andy had said, I had been able to see quite clearly that there had been no-one else on the pathway and that I wasn't being followed. No outsider would have known I was going there and there was nothing to connect me to Andy's people either, only Andy himself.

As I turned onto the motorway that would take me to Linda's I experienced only one negative twinge, and I was aware that it had come rather late. No matter how indirect my relationship was with the criminals who must be behind this work, in practical terms I had become one of them. But what I had become had to be weighed against what I had been, I told myself, I had to keep a balanced view. I wasn't doing this for fun.

It should take me about half an hour to get to Linda's, I calculated from the map, and by the time I had reached the main road my thoughts on the rights and wrongs of what I was doing had given way to those concerning the relationship I hoped to have with her.

If she had been a golfer then things might have been easier, I reflected not too seriously, but I knew that that would have been asking for too much. And anyway, a lot of golfers, probably most of them for that matter, didn't make off with woman golfers. What else might I have in common with her? I wondered. Maybe if she had liked Chopin that would have helped. I could have impressed her with my playing, in spite of my large bony hands, like some elderly piano teacher might do when hammering out a short, loud and spectacular excerpt from a great piece before the student's parents, knowing full well that a performance of the whole piece or even half of it was well beyond their present capabilities. I could have played Liszt's 'Liebestraum' with certain difficult passages left out, or one of Chopin's own favourites, 'The Revolutionary Etude', whose power and volume were inclined to drown out the mistakes. I could even have managed 'Rhapsody in Blue' if I had shrunk some of the difficult chords to suit my lack of technical expertise. But then again would these musical stars have shone so brightly in Linda's firmament as they did in mine? Were they really the kind of help that I needed to strike up a serious relationship with her? They weren't, I finally realised. The huge obstacle, and I was beginning to see it as that now, which lay in my path if I was to get anywhere with Linda was not that we didn't have very much in common. It was something which went much deeper than this. It was a world view, no less, her father's world-view and, whether I liked it or not, I would have to come to terms with it, try to understand it, so that I could relate, in the way that I hoped, with the woman who shared it with him.

At first the effect of his sermons had been similar to that which was often experienced when listening to someone on the radio enthuse over a subject you were unfamiliar with, where the incomprehensible whole nevertheless contained snatches you could understand and appreciate. Although, of course, you could always turn the radio off.

Gradually and surprisingly, however, he had begun to catch my attention and I hadn't wanted to switch him off so often. His thoughts on Noah, for instance, were worth paying some attention to when the benefits of the multi-cultural society were being lauded by so many people these days.

Not so with the Pastor, however. National barriers and racial distinctions proceeded from God, according to him, Who divides and compartmentalise the human race rather than communises it. The idea of one community of men, one family of human beings just wasn't on. It wasn't in the natural order of things, he would strongly contend, and in the long run no good would ever come of it.

With the Pastor you didn't have to go as far back as Adam or get lost in space with some scientific theory, to see the significance of the fact that 'just as it was in the days of Noah …' so might it very well be in our own days too when global warming intensifies and the climate changes for the worse.

It wasn't too difficult to understand how he thought that mankind was headed in the wrong direction, down rather than up, and that the glorious scientifically induced future of the evolutionists didn't seem to be getting any nearer. It was good that I could see there might be at least a modicum of truth in all this. I had to, if I wanted to get anywhere with Linda.

But to do this I would have to get my facts right, or rather her facts. To her the book of Genesis was history, plain and simple, and the Great Flood was a starting off point for many of her beliefs.

The Flood had been God's judgement on the whole human race living at that time, all of whom, apart from Noah and his family, were drowned and swept away. After The Flood, according to her, Noah's three sons had founded the original 58 nations. Shem, produced 20, Ham 26 and Japheth 12.

Getting lost when she had added a few more – Israel from Abram, the Moabites and Ammonites from Lot, Ishmaelites from Ishmael, and Edomites from Esau – I could nevertheless see what she was driving at. Man had been divided up, not joined up.

*

My beautiful history teacher, for surely that's what she really was, stood in the doorway of the manse wearing plain anorak and jeans, but still with a distinctive look about her, her attractiveness undiminished.

"Dad says I've to give you his regards", she told me apologetically. "He'd to go down to the Hall."

We drove along the Shore Road for a few miles and, as I drove past the entrance to one of the many caravan parks in the area, I spotted Steve driving out in a workshop van. I was glad that he didn't see us. I wanted to keep my relationship with Linda separate from my friendship with Andy and the others. She wouldn't have anything in common with them, apart from the fact that she knew me, of course.

After a while we crossed a hump-backed bridge and parked in a lay-by which overlooked the bay. The tide was coming in, accompanied by a strong breeze, and huge waves sprinkled with surf were crashing onto the beach.

The sea had been calm when I had, on that other occasion, walked along the shore with Karen, I remembered, thinking how appropriate that had been, now that I was here with

Linda. There had been nothing at stake then. Karen had belonged to Andy, not to me.

And here, although Linda didn't belong to me either, I thought the turbulent scene well-suited to the challenge and uncertainty present in our relationship.

"What did your father say about me turning up again?" I asked her, as we left the car.

"Not much," she said, obviously not wanting to give me a direct answer.

"And are you working somewhere in this area now?" she asked, as we settled in a sheltered spot in which there were some rocks we could comfortably sit on.

"No. I came here to see you, that's all," I told her bravely.

"Seriously John," she protested, still smiling but avoiding my eyes.

"I am being serious."

"You came to see me," she repeated. "And that's the only reason?"

"It is. Have I done the wrong thing?" I asked her, aware that the conversation was going in a familiar direction, and that once more the hopes I had about her feelings for me could be dashed so easily by her answer.

"I suppose not," she answered, still avoiding my eyes, her smile fading.

"Suppose?" I ventured hopefully.

"Yes. I'm glad you've come all this way just to see me," she said, looking up and speaking in a stronger tone of voice.

But the feeling of relief her answer engendered was to be short-lived.

"But you know we still have a problem, don't you?" she said, at once unnerving me again. I hadn't meant the conversation to be as all-inclusive as this. It was too soon.

"Which particular problem?" I asked, as if I didn't know.

"You know what my father is like?"

"I have a great respect for your father, Linda, you know that," I told her, immediately on the defensive.

"I know you have John. But that's not really the point is it? Most people respect him, don't they?"

I hadn't expected this, although, of course, I knew it wasn't the point. But I didn't feel ready to face up to what was.

"Linda, I'm sorry I don't seem to fit in too well," I struggled.

"You don't have to apologise, John. I just thought it was better to get this particular matter out into the open, that's all."

She was right, from her point of view, but definitely not from mine. She was her father's daughter and it would be unrealistic to expect her to go against him. Bringing up my hesitancy about things concerning the Church, or the Bible would be inclined to bring me into conflict with her father's ideas which I had every reason to think would be no mean task.

To the Pastor, the popular and widespread denials of the truth upon which atheists and agnostics depend on so heavily were themselves just as easy to deny or refute. People don't or can't believe the miracles of the Bible and yet they are surrounded everyday by miraculous happenings, e.g. in the field of electronics etc. and they don't doubt any of them for a minute. They disbelieve that their every word and deed can be recorded and that the consequences of their actions can be held against them on the Day of Judgement, and yet their medical records, present whereabouts, and very much else about them is presently being recorded electronically, with ease and precision, by mere men.

As often happened, I felt I could almost go along with this assertion for not so long ago the awe inspiring sight of Emperor Ming and Flash Gordon, conversing face to face on a 'visual telephone' had been thought of as a miracle by cinema audiences. They weren't just conversing on the telephone, which audiences at that time had thought to be clever enough, not everyone had a telephone, they could actually see each other, too.

But going along with some of the things the Pastor taught wouldn't be enough, I knew. Not nearly enough.

It's just that Dad thinks I should only get involved with people who more or less believe what we believe Linda said, as if reading my mind, and you know how he can support everything with Scripture," she added, frowning at me gently.

"His interpretation of Scripture, you mean," I commented boldly, but without conviction.

"You definitely don't go along with Dad all the way, John, do you?" she said, in what I realised was to her a very serious challenge.

"In most things I do, Linda. I just have problems here and there."

"Well I don't always agree with him either," she said, still in a conciliatory tone. "But with sixty six books in the Bible, written in a variety of literary forms, I suppose there's bound to be differences of opinion somewhere, isn't there?"

"Of course there is," I hastily agreed, guiltily aware that my thoughts were pulling me in another direction.

As I looked across at her, sitting with poise on a rock she made look like a piece of furniture, I tried to put out of my mind the great promise contained in the view I had of her ankles, and to resist the temptation to let my thoughts wander up beyond her knees.

"There's a lot of truth in what you say, Linda, but give me an example of where we might be at complete loggerheads?" I asked, giving her something to occupy her mind, while I tried to suppress thoughts of what I imagined would be soft, ample thighs enclosing those parts of her body that I felt ashamed to be thinking about during a conversation like this.

"The Scriptures say, 'Be ye not unequally yoked,'" she stated, instantly lowering my temperature. She had gone right to the point, again.

"Could you put that another way?" I asked, finally realising I would have to concentrate my attention on what she thought was the right subject, not on the one I wished it was.

True believers should not get too involved, or whatever else, with unbelievers, or people with funny ideas."

"Funny ideas? You mean me?" I asked uneasily.

"Not quite – they're people who say they believe in the Bible but really have another Bible, specially rewritten to suit them, concealed behind their back. Like some of the sects, for instance."

"That's definitely not me."

"It's not," she agreed. "I didn't quite mean that."

Her face wore a sympathetic look which I wasn't happy with. Was she being patronising without meaning to be, I wondered.

If she was, maybe she was entitled to be. I believed everything and yet nothing while she knew exactly where she stood on this subject. Her eyes and her lips were her most noticeable features, now that I had abandoned the others, and I was making the most of them. I thought of pressing my lips against hers and of her large brown eyes closing in surrender. If I could harbour such thoughts during a conversation of this kind, wasn't she entitled to feel superior? I asked myself despairingly.

"I envy you, Linda," I heard myself say.

"Envy?"

"Yes. You're so sure about what you believe. With me, so many things are controversial."

"Controversy can sometimes be challenging," she commented.

I thought of taking her in my arms, and again of pressing my lips against hers. This would be controversial, and challenging, I told myself, feeling even more ashamed than ever of my ability to put what in the circumstances were debasing, even adolescent thoughts, out of my mind.

"Controversy can be confusing, just as often as it is challenging, Linda," I replied, making a further effort to justify my thoughts on the subject.

"Give me an example then," she asked.

I almost gave up at that point. In spite of all my efforts to the contrary I could see that our opinions would just have to differ which would be better than merely lusting after her, as I had been doing, I told myself.

"I'm a British soldier fighting the Japanese in the jungle, in the Second World War," I began, falling back as usual on something from the Book Collection.

"Okay".

"You'll know of course, what the Japanese soldiers were like at that time."

"I do, and you're going to say something about turning the other cheek, and loving your enemy, etc," she said, wrongly anticipating my line of thought.

"Far from it."

Although she looked unpleasantly surprised at this, I felt I had to go on.

"I'm going to say that dropping the atom bomb was a very good idea."

"You mean they were right to drop the atom bomb and kill thousands of defenceless civilians?"

How many times had I heard this? How could killing defenceless civilians ever sound right? Did she think I was stupid?

"I can't quite say that, Linda."

"Well?"

"Well. That's the problem. The British soldier is a civilian too, isn't he? He didn't volunteer. He was called up."

"Weren't the Japanese going to surrender anyway?"

"After that soldier got killed, and maybe a few hundred thousand others, even far more than that probably."

"And what about the children incinerated in the blast?" she asked, dismissive of my assertion.

"And what about the soldier's children? I countered. The ones who won't be born at all, if the bomb isn't dropped."

Could I blame her for thinking like this, for not seeing my difficulty? How could she identify with a soldier facing death in the jungle? But was I any better? How could I identify with people like her, people who had been brought up in the Church and whose whole way of life revolved around it? As had become the practice these days, point of view, hers in this case, was going to gain the advantage and be taken for the absolute truth. The atom bomb would have to be bad.

"Principle and practice are further apart for me than they are for you, Linda. That's all I'm saying."

"Okay, we're equal. You don't understand me and I don't understand you," she said, in a playful tone that sounded forced, indicating as I had feared, that I had made my point unwisely from an overall point of view.

"Well if dropping the bomb was all that bad then the people behind it won't go unpunished will they, at least not according to your father they won't?"

"You don't believe that either do you?" she said accusingly.

"Believe what?"

"In the absolute sovereignty of God."

"That God is still on the throne you mean."

"There's no need to be flippant", she chided.

The look on her face confirmed that what I had feared all along had actually happened. Once I started to contradict her in any serious way and appear to cast doubt on what she believed then our relationship would suffer.

"You've misunderstood me", I lied. "Of course I believe in the sovereignty of God."

"But not that God still deals with people and nations in the same way as he did in The Old Testament?"

If this was anything like a lover's tiff then it was too much for me, I thought. She was deadly serious about all this, just like her father. I was on dangerous ground. I had to very quickly get things back to where I felt they had been before we got out of the car.

"You're taking me the wrong way Linda", I pleaded. "I'm not really disagreeing with you. It's just that I'm not so well read on the subject as you are."

"Well what don't you know?"

She was definitely being patronising now, I could see. I wasn't sure if I liked her more, or less, for this but it didn't effect how I felt about her, which was more important right then.

"That's maybe a bit too much to discuss right now", I said meekly.

"What about a walk?" I added as a means of escape, looking along the shore to where I could see a path that had been trodden into the grassy verge which sloped down to the sheltered spot in which we were sitting.

We had to make our way over the rocks to get there and she reached out to me several times to steady herself, always taking her arm away when she had regained her balance. I managed to grip her arm as we negotiated the final rock, and we reached the pathway hand in hand.

We walked for a while, the strong wind coming in from the sea making conversation difficult. My thoughts flitted over what we had been discussing, as if reliving a job interview. Would the opposing views I had expressed during my attempts to escape from my lewd thoughts bring about my downfall.

The pathway led us away from the shore and out of the wind where I noticed her hair was rich enough in texture to have withstood the onslaught of the weather and the colour had risen in her cheeks.

That she continued to hold my hand I hoped might signify that no serious harm had been done, here at least, by the dropping of the atom bomb, or by our brief reference to God's intervention in human affairs. Encouraged by this, I slipped my arm around her waist, gently pulling her closer to me, as we walked.

Pleased at the progress indicated by her lack of resistance, I felt I had to make the most of it before we reached the end of the pathway. I stopped and, when she turned to look up at me, I placed my other arm on her shoulder and pulled her round to face me. I felt her thighs press against mine.

I knew it wouldn't be easy to get past her anorak and jeans. I would have as much chance as the weather had. I was glad that the idea of doing so was a desire rather than an intention and was at first content to press my cheek against hers, feeling her warm breath on my ear.

But before long I felt like kissing her on the lips and was even having thoughts about what might lie ahead if I attempted to reach the universal destination by negotiating the breasts, thighs and panties likely to be met, in that order, along the way. Would some people never learn.

Compared to some of the other thoughts that had been running through my mind kissing her didn't seem much but now I couldn't bring myself to do even this. Behaving towards her in this way in this place didn't seem right. But I drew her in closer to me, nevertheless.

"Someone will see us," she said, pulling away from me, looking up and down the pathway.

She didn't seem too put out by what I had actually done, only by the risk we ran of being seen.

Since I had only pressed against her, and she couldn't have known of the other more ambitious thoughts she had inspired in me, I realised I was missing the point. It wasn't her response, the fact that she was a woman in spite of her beliefs, which was the issue here, it was my attitude. I didn't feel comfortable with the idea of pushing her off the pathway into the bushes where no-one might see us, and where the objects of desire hidden under her anorak and jeans might be revealed to me. From the event in the ante room at the Annual Staff Dance, surely I had learned something, that behaviour of this kind could have unfortunate, long-term consequences. On this occasion I was going to pay heed to the particular 'Keep off the Grass' sign that I felt had been put up by the fact she was the Pastor's daughter. But at least I could look forward to my next move, whatever that was going to be, without feeling that I had spoiled anything.

The fact that my relationship with her was a bit like fighting a war on two fronts was something that didn't occur to me until very much later which, in view of that great devastating example cited in the Book Collection of Germany attacking Russia in 1941 before it had beaten Britain, was just as well.

chapter
seventeen

As I drove along the dual carriageway on the second run, I calculated that I would be at my destination in under an hour, and that I would be there for about ten minutes. Allowing for unexpected delays and the fact that some of the journeys would be at the far end of the fifty mile radius I was at this point expected to work within, the cash payment plus petrol allowance was generous, to say the least. I would have to sell at least ten extinguishers to earn that much in commission. I didn't have to remind myself that it would take a lot more than a few hours to do that, and a lot more effort too. If I could do these deliveries once or twice a week, it wouldn't be long before I could take a wad of banknotes out of a long brown envelope with as much ease as Andy had.

But this work had its difficulties too. On one occasion there were three cars behind me, keeping pace with me, and I had had to pull off the road to let them go past. I hadn't been sure if had been doing the right thing or if I had just been letting my nerves get the better of me again?

Soon I was on a coast road where the many bends reduced my field of vision. Although I had to give a little more attention to my driving I was enjoying the pleasant view I had of the sea, but the occasional glimpse I got of some car or other travelling at what appeared to be a fixed distance behind me, kept reminding me that I was only being paid so much because I was doing something I shouldn't be, and that there was bound to be a risk of some sort attached to it.

When I reached the town I hadn't gone far along the main road when I saw, in the rear view mirror, a car that had been coming along behind me, turn off into a side street, leaving me with a clear view of the empty approach road I had just come down. Everything was going to be all right, I told myself, feeling greatly relieved.

The black Rover with the right registration plate was easy to spot, too. Taking out the keys Andy had given me, I laid them on the passenger seat, drawing into the side of the road about twenty yards or so beyond the vehicle, and calmly got out.

There were several people on both sides of the street, none of whom gave me the enquiring or challenging look that residents would usually give to newcomers. They would be passers-by, I supposed, certainly not people lying in wait for me.

I laid the package on the back seat of the Rover and took out the one that was already there, putting it on the roof as I re-locked the door, resisting a strong impulse to look up an down the street as I strolled back to my car.

As I headed towards the outskirts of the town I felt pleased with myself. My nerves hadn't let me down, after all. Once more I had done what had been expected of me. But as soon as I reached the dual carriageway my nervousness returned. The success or failure of what I was doing, I grimly reflected, wouldn't depend on how reliable I was but on whether or not I actually was being followed. And what if I was? And who by? Andy had never even brought this up. Should he have? I was definitely out of my depth in all this.

But I wasn't being followed. Every vehicle that came up behind me eventually overtook me until at last there was nothing but the empty road stretching endlessly behind me. I felt annoyed that the job was taking so much out of me. If I wasn't being followed, then what was I worrying about? I didn't even know if there was anything harmful in the package, for that matter.

But using my ignorance of its contents to lessen my anxiety didn't work for long. I had it in my possession and that alone could probably get me in to serious trouble. And it wasn't only that. There was something else. As I looked again in the rear view mirror, I knew that the strong feeling of relief I felt at once more seeing an empty road wasn't going to be enough to make me feel really happy at what I was doing.

It wasn't the actual nature of the crime which was bothering me. After all, I wasn't a murderer, or a kidnapper. Their souls definitely belonged on the other side of that great divide which separates absolute evil from mere breaking of the law. Mine didn't.

As I glanced over my shoulder at the package lying on the back set it dawned on me that what was really bothering me was quite simple. It was the fact that I wasn't just involved with criminals, I actually was one now. It was no use pleading that I hadn't thought the crime up, or set it in motion, for how many crimes had only became possible because of the help given by accomplices? And didn't they always downplay their role just like I was doing?

Hadn't the Book Collection drawn my attention to the professed innocence of the drivers of the trains which had pulled cattle trucks crammed full of suffocating people to the Nazi death camps? Or the guards in other camps, only obeying orders, when they had forced prisoners to go to their deaths hauling heavy stones up a hill? Didn't evil always fully reproduce itself in the hearts of its helpers? And didn't they always plead otherwise on the day of reckoning?

But was I being fair to myself? All things considered, I wasn't merely acquiescing in Andy's offer of a job, like someone giving in to temptation, I was desperate.

If I didn't get money from somewhere then not only would I lose the flat, with all that that entailed but, even worse, I would have to stand by helplessly as Aunt Grace was moved out of the private nursing home to join me on my way down the ladder. I had to do something to stop these things happening. Surely my conscience shouldn't be bothering me too much.

But conscience wasn't the final arbiter, I had once heard the Pastor declare. You had to go a bit deeper than that if you wanted to resolve any uncertainty you might have about what was right and what was wrong. Weren't very evil men capable of having a good night's sleep? he would ask.

Although I had doubts about some of the things he said with such apparent authority, I hoped, for his sake, that it wasn't true, as Alexis De Tocqueville, the great 19th century French historian had said in the Book Collection, that no man can struggle to advantage against the spirit of the age, for I was beginning to see that this was the kind of struggle which the Pastor was actually involved in, but perhaps more significantly, if I was absolutely honest with myself, the beliefs that underpinned his world view were gradually becoming things I was giving some weight to in my own struggle, too. His beliefs had made a much deeper impression on me than I thought.

The way he had justified his uncompromising stance on issues I had long since thought dead had certainly made me sit up and think. Giving in to his suggestion that I go back and re-examine some of these old-fashioned beliefs didn't necessarily mean that I had was being got at, like a convert to the teachings of some ridiculous cult, I had reasoned with myself at the time.

But what then was the true nature of what I was being drawn into that could so effect my way of looking at things, even when it looked like I wasn't going to get caught? In what way was the Pastor's world view cutting into my own? Maybe if I could get to the bottom of this I would feel a good bit better about myself.

To him, for a start, the planet wasn't just suspended in space with the human race being left, or always having been, on its own, to face the diverse threats to its existence. Indeed, many of these very threats, according to him, were directly connected to what he saw as the hand of an almighty God on human affairs which, in the way he told it, seemed a bit more than just an old fashioned fear of God. Even the climate change he had used to introduce the subject was topical.

The Bible, as he had pointed out so often, was replete with passages in which certain natural disasters, similar to those occurring today, were described as punishments for wrong doing, meted out to countries and peoples whose conduct was contrary to an exacting divine standard.

The list he had recited was easy to remember and included floods, famines, storms, earthquakes, insect pests, and diseases, to which he had added those other scourges – war, unemployment and loss of economic prosperity, attributing all of these to the same root cause.

And to make matters worse it wasn't as though 'modern man' hadn't been warned, he had pointed out, just as much as man had been warned in Noah's day and afterwards, as Linda was always saying. That the apostles were quite few in number, as was commonly thought, and couldn't have reached all that many people with their message, was something he strongly refuted. Paul was only one of thousands who had spread the message to the far corners of the world. There were hundreds of churches in North Africa, for example, in the 2nd Century, and in Mongolia a little later. The heathenism which pervades many parts of the globe was more often than not attributable to a rejection of the truth which had been delivered at an earlier period in history, according to him.

If all this was an integral part of the Pastor's world-view then how did my own world-view relate to it and how were his ideas eating into mine.

Or, perhaps more to the point, did I really have a world-view worthy of the name? Wasn't I really just an observer pleased to gain an occasional insight of some kind from one of my books. But no, his ideas did supplant mine, I could see. For if many of these great events I had read of in the Book Collection had indeed been influenced by various kinds of divine intervention then this showed history up in a very different light from the one I had grown used to.

Was the calm sea at Dunkirk heaven sent to allow the bulk of the British Army in France and some of its allies to escape the Germans. Was the Battle of Britain won by the Royal Air Force alone, or was the victory also decided at a much higher altitude. Was France, with all its huge armies, defeated by the Germans in a few days because of a non-military intervention?

Even if the Scriptures were writings of less than divine origin, as his opponents would say, the many excerpts he used as examples of divine intervention had more than a ring of truth to them. The actual events themselves were often recorded in the history books of the period, too, and the explanations he gave for their occurrence sounded appropriate, regardless of whether or not his sources were inspired.

To dismiss out of hand the connection he made between the catastrophes that befell certain nations and the great wrongs they had committed I now felt was unreasonable. Would anyone say that Gibbon was automatically wrong about the Rise and Fall of the Roman Empire just because he, like the Pastor, hadn't actually witnessed the events and was without a certain kind of proof.

Was it all that far-fetched to say that the Syrian leaders in days of old had lost their power and that their people were enslaved because they slaughtered the population of Gilead. And that Tyre, Nineveh and Babylon fell because they conducted their business affairs dishonestly. Were these assertions not even worthy of being given a hearing?

When he split up the various kinds of national misdemeanours that God so thoroughly disapproved of into three groups – political, religious and moral – to my surprise almost every example he quoted from the ancient world brought to mind similar behaviour on the part of several countries as recently as just before, during and after the two World Wars.

In fact, so easy to recognise in recent history were the kind of misdemeanours he described that I could recite them from memory.

Those of a political nature were:

+ Breaking treaties.
+ Committing atrocities.
+ Undermining the government of other countries.
+ Being ruthless towards those seen as enemies.
+ Being aggressive towards other countries to promote own national self-interest.

+ Lacking sympathy for countries in trouble.
+ Being arrogant because of one's industrial might and power.
+ Plundering fallen nations.
+ Slaughtering the innocent to achieve military gains.

Those of a religious nature:

> (These were more controversial since the right to indulge in some of them would be upheld today, even applauded, by many people holding 'liberal' or 'liberalising' views.)

+ Bending the truth to accommodate immoral behaviour.
+ Allowing false teaching to be freely disseminated.
+ Scorning the advice given by religious leaders.
+ Indulging in pagan practices and making false claims for them.
+ Adoring and worshipping men instead of their creator.

And finally, those concerning morals:

> (As for the evils committed within this group, so ingrained and widespread were they, he declared, that most of them wouldn't even be recognised for what they are.)

+ Being ungrateful for the fact that all basic needs were being met.
+ Pining after a life of luxury and self-indulgence.
+ Allowing dishonest commercial practices to become the order of the day.

- Being lethargic and indifferent to very important national issues.
- Encouraging vanity to the point of absurdity in women.
- Approving, even applauding, various kinds of immorality.

It wasn't just the Pastor's ability to clearly identify these misdemeanours that had so impressed me, it was the skill with which he could place the events, both the crime and the punishment, in a realistic historical setting.

The opposing point of view in which the wayward instincts of man, which drove him to these extremities, would be gradually rendered harmless as civilisation advanced, without any need of a divine regulator, sounded good but there was absolutely no sign of its being true. As I thought again of some of the evils described on the Pastor's list and of my own petty little transgression in making these deliveries I knew at last what it was that was really bothering me. To do something and know you would never be found out was one thing, but to know that a day of judgement would definitely dawn and that all your acts were being observed, recorded and measured was a simple restraint of great magnitude, not just effecting the human race as a whole but bearing down, right at this minute, on me.

Only going to Church in the first place to please Aunt Grace, and after that mainly because of Linda, I was now reciting the Pastor's list of political, religious and moral sins as if my life depended on it. There was no doubt the pressure was taking its toll. I was beginning to develop a genuine and heartfelt fear of God, in spite of my otherwise worldly view of life.

I pulled into a lay-by to gather my thoughts and clear my mind, parking at the opening, on this occasion, so that I could better see the occupants of any cars that might pull in beside me.

The rays from that 'far distant heavenly body' were once again heating up the inside of the car but in spite of the heat and the lack of fresh air my head began to clear. The significance of the blinding light caused by the sun shining directly onto the bonnet of the car didn't escape me.

Who were the Pastor's opponents? I had to ask myself again, the people whose views I no longer found so convincing. For the most part, I felt, they seemed to be people who would propel your thoughts back millions of years in support of their ideas, along a highway strewn with signposts marked Science in large print but with the words, Assumption, Possibility and Probability, in very small print, written underneath.

The Pastor, in introducing me to the basic tenets of his world view hadn't had to go back nearly as far as these scientists. With him, for practical purposes, it had all started at the Flood. What Flood? I remember asking myself at the time. Surely he meant the local ones. That he had meant a world-wide one, had come as a surprise. How could he still believe this?

That none of the geological evidence for or against this world-wide flood was considered to be conclusive surprised me even more. He wasn't flying in the face of all the facts, after all.

But how could someone in this day and age attempt to turn the story of Noah into a main line issue, I couldn't help asking myself once more, when it was really a topic suitable for children's books?

Easy, according to the Pastor. Hadn't Christ himself wholeheartedly endorsed it? Wasn't that reason enough? he had asked. Throwing out the story of Noah and The Flood meant, at the same time, disposing of the moral judgement that lay behind it and that, from his point of view, said it all. Man wanted the freedom to do anything he wanted. He didn't want such things as divine restraining orders to hinder him or other divine enactments which might call him to account. Not only did they not exist, they weren't needed. Man was quite capable of sorting things out himself, even if there was little real evidence of it.

But surely the number of war dead, even in recent times, killed in action or otherwise removed from the scene of time, suggested that man was beyond self-help. How could 'civilised' man purport to place such a high value on a single human life and yet so frequently find a reason to destroy it en masse. That organised religion had often mishandled, even manhandled its application of the divine edicts he was willing to admit, but that didn't annul them. It was just that they weren't wanted.

But wanted or not, he had gone on, they are there just the same and just as surely as God has set up the Law of Nature by which fruit falls from the tree and fire burns the finger, the former making even the premier league footballer tumble to the ground and the latter the professional fire fighter run for his life, so has he set up the Moral Law with different but just as certain means of enforcement.

Like the above Law of Nature which the footballer and fire fighter are so respectful of, so is the Moral Law, often in a less immediate and therefore less obvious way, exerting its full force on those who have chosen to disregard it.

'This is God's world, not man's,' I remembered him saying. 'And while man can often choose his actions, he can't, in the same way, choose the results of these actions.' According to him, any man who thought he could disregard the Moral Law with impunity was a moral imbecile. As I drove along the dual carriageway with nothing in my rear view mirror to disturb my thoughts I felt, with inescapable finality, that all this applied to me.

It was impossible to ignore it. Whether I had been got at, persuaded or enlightened was academic and didn't alter the overall effect his ideas were having on me. What the Pastor said wouldn't go away.

And, even if there did seem to be pieces missing from his world view, the extent to which I nevertheless felt able to subscribe to it was enough. Although I wasn't pleased with the suddenness of my about-face I knew that, come what may, I had to completely sever my connection with the work I was doing for Andy, and with the men who were behind it. It didn't matter what it made me look like. I wasn't just having cold feet, and even if I was it wasn't for the usual reason. It wasn't a question of getting caught. Deep within me I felt I had been caught already.

Pleased that I had made a firm and clear decision, albeit for a seemingly very old fashioned reason, the fear of God, and that the fear of God was said to be the beginning of wisdom, I began to enjoy the drive. I realised that the cars behind me were unlikely to be following me for 'right' was now very much on my side.

But the strong feeling of relief gradually slipped away as I wondered what I was going to say to Andy.

chapter eighteen

In spite of all my soul-searching I found it hard to put out of my mind the fact that the envelope Andy had given me, containing my cash payment, represented the only real progress I had made in my efforts to solve my financial problems. I slipped the envelope into my pocket and sat back in a chair outside the caravan to consider the best way of telling him about my decision to give up the work. It was going to be a lot harder to say 'no' than it had been to say 'yes'.

Unexpectedly, Andy slid another envelope across the table and onto my lap.

"This one's a nuisance," he said. "It's a job I want to get out of the way."

"Oh right," I muttered, before I had managed to tell him about what was on my mind.

"Big Tom's away and you're the only one available to do this run," he added. "I'm glad you're here, John."

I lifted up the envelope, hesitating as I was about to tuck it into my pocket beside the other one. I didn't want to go back on my decision but I didn't want to let Andy down either.

"And I thought I'd better tell you, John," he said, again before I could find the right words, "I'm leaving Bartons. I'll be out of this hell-hole in a few days," he declared, with a broad grin on his face.

"You mean this is going to be my last job?" I asked, relieved at first that I might not after all have to tell him I had decided not to continue with the work but suddenly and sadly aware of the fact that this might also bring to an end the evenings in the Old Toll Bar and the weekends at the caravan. Were Karen, Big Tom, Liz, all going to vanish into a way of life I was no longer a part of?

"Of course it won't be your last job," Andy answered. "The deliveries won't be affected just because I'm leaving Bartons. Don't worry, John, your future is secure with me," he went on, affecting the authoritative but kindly tone of a benevolent employer, and then grinning in his usual way.

I wasn't surprised. His words only confirmed what I already knew. Andy wasn't the kind of person who let you down. It was me who had been about to walk out on him. If he needed me for this run, then I was going to do it.

"Will you still be working in Fire Protection?" I asked him, feeling that I was entitled to an explanation, of some sort at least.

"Hardly," he replied, scowling.

That his answer suggested he might not want to take me into his confidence disappointed me, but I tried not to show it.

"I suppose you're wondering what this is all about?" he asked, now saying exactly what I wanted to hear and what I had learned to expect from him. The conversation always seemed to flow like this when I was talking to him. With Andy, there were never any subtle undertones that made you suspect his motives. He was always straight with you, someone you could trust, and if he held anything back deceit was never a part of it.

"To be honest, Andy, I am wondering," I admitted. "What kind of business are we in?" I asked, hoping I could at least get a few things cleared up. What were we actually doing? What kind of criminal was I?

"Well it's not drugs, John, in case that's what you're thinking. It's often just money. You know, transactions you don't want to record."

"Laundering?"

"Sometimes, but sometimes just payments for services rendered. That kind of thing. It's just a back to basics and much safer way of doing business, that's all. But we're into something much bigger now," he added enthusiastically.

"And that's why you're leaving Bartons?"

"It's something to do with it. Up to now I've been a kind of transport manager. I organise the runs, make sure everything gets from A to B, and sometimes do a bit of heavy stuff if it's needed."

"Heavy stuff?"

"A spin off from the army," he further explained. I was in Special Forces for five years with Big Tom. When we came out I set up a security company down south. The Operation made me an offer, and here I am, a good bit safer than I was in the army, at least for most of the time, and with a lot more money to spend."

His features wore that faintly amused expression that had impressed me so much when I first met him. I always warmed to it. When it faded there seemed to be something quite different, formidable and unrelenting, lying just underneath the surface. To be trusted by someone like him meant a lot to me.

"I shouldn't really be telling you this, John," he went on. "But the people I work for are taking over the Casino. That's mainly why I'm up here."

"And where do fire extinguishers fit into all this?" I asked him, hungry for more information. "What have Bartons got to do with it?"

Andy laughed. "Fair question, John. The answer is, well, not all that much. I learnt about extinguishers in the army."

"They're just a cover?"

"In this business everything has to be very low profile, John, and with the Casino about to become a part of it, it's got to be even more so. There's a lot of brains on both sides of the law these days and we've got to go about things in a different way. That's where people like you fit in."

"Like me?"

"You can be trusted, John, and you've got your head screwed on," he said, patting me on the back.

"And you even look educated," he added, smiling, and patting me even harder. "You're just what we're looking for."

"A respectable front, you mean," I commented, trying to sound worldly wise.

"I know men, John. We've got to have the right kind of people working for us these days and we're willing to pay good money to get them."

How right I had been about him all along was now plainly obvious. He didn't belong in Bartons. Andy was much more than this. Although he had scruples of a certain kind, of course he had, it was obvious he wouldn't be tied down, like I was, by principles and beliefs that always had to be taken into account before anything could get done. But he would look out for his friends. Big Tom, for example, hung on his every word. It was just that, with Andy, I could see how the quickest way of dealing with something would always take priority over the rights and wrongs of it. A problem would be an obstacle that had to be overcome at once, rather than an issue that had to be considered. I wondered where he would fit into the Pastor's scheme of things. There had to be a place for people like him there somewhere, surely.

In admiring him in this way, and going back on my decision to give this work up, was I beginning to think like a criminal again? Surely not. Didn't many otherwise Godly men get into a similar position when they were engaged in what they thought was a just war, uttering up prayers for the success of their mission as they mowed down the enemy. Although the Pastor's world view might ultimately be the right one didn't many of the acts committed by good men sometimes chip it a little along the edges? Apparently not all saints felt they could or should be conscientious objectors. Some wars just had to be fought. Maybe I could use this as an excuse, too, for wasn't I at war? If I couldn't get money to pay my debts then I would go under. Should the main issue really be that what I was doing for Andy was against the law or, like the dropping of the atom bomb was said to have been, wasn't the end more important than the means?

The money I was being paid by Andy meant I could hold on to the flat and that Grace could remain safely in the Home, and that I didn't have to throw up my hands in despair, not just yet. The Pastor's elevated world view could surely be adjusted to accommodate this. I wasn't going against all that he stood for, it was the circumstances that were all wrong. Sitting in the pew was one thing, standing with your back to the wall was another.

In my plight Andy and his friends had been light out of the darkness. They had accepted me, treated me as if I was one of them. All of them in different ways seemed to have strong blood running through their veins and for the short time I had known them I had begun to feel that I had too. Their strength had rubbed off on me, and kept me going.

Making these deliveries was wrong and I was right in worrying about what it might lead to. But wasn't hoisting the white flag wrong too. Where else was I going to get the money I needed to survive? Could I afford to have a world view that didn't take things like this into account?

The delivery was important to Andy and, for that reason, it was important to me, too. Andy didn't let you down and I wasn't going to let him down either. He needed me for this delivery, and I was going to do it for this reason and not because I was desperate for the money. It was as simple as that.

*

BUT I HAD LEFT ANDY DOWN AFTER ALL, SITTING THERE IN THE LAY-BY DRINKING TEA, ALLOWING THE SMILING MAN TO CREEP UP ON ME. WHERE WAS I IN THE BOOK COLLECTION NOW? WHICH OF THE GREAT ERRORS THAT WERE SO WELL DOCUMENTED THERE HAD I COMMITTED THAT COULD BRING ME FULL CIRCLE TO YET ANOTHER ABJECT FAILURE? HAD I BEEN CARELESS, WRONG-HEADED, ARROGANT, IGNORANT OR WAS I JUST A VICTIM OF BAD LUCK OR HUMAN FRAILTY?

In spite of all this, and what Andy had said might happen, I gradually began to feel a bit better. Sitting here in the car with Karen, heading out to confront Steve and the smiling man, two professional criminals, with a gun in my pocket, and my life expectancy considerably reduced, didn't seem all that bad. At least I was doing the very best I could. Since leaving the Food Importers I had always seemed to be on the wrong

end of things and filled with self-deprecating introspection.
It couldn't be that way now. There wasn't time. I had lost the
Package and, at all costs, I was going to get it back.

I definitely couldn't afford to sit here in my usual way
wishing I could put the clock back. In the real world the clock
only went forward and I had to get on top of these events
before I was overcome by them.

Whether I liked it or not, I wasn't a salesman in this world,
or an amateur theologian. I was a criminal, and I had to be
prepared to act like one if I was to have any chance of success.

"We're almost there," Karen said. "It's just round the corner."

I pulled over and turned to face her.

"You're not going into the caravan park, Karen," I told her.

"I thought that's what I was here for?" she replied
indignantly. "It's a big park. Do you think you'll find these
people by just wandering about?"

Regardless of her attitude, however, I still felt responsible
for her safety. I couldn't bear the thought of anything
happening to her. She might belong to Andy, but right now
it was me who was the man in her life, even if it wouldn't be
for long.

"Well come as far as you have to, point out to me which
caravan it is, then come right back to the car," I told her
brusquely.

"You're really quite at home with all this, aren't you," she
said, with the glimmer of a smile on her lips. "Barking out
orders and carrying a gun."

She looked composed and her voice was strong and clear.

"Are you absolutely sure we're going about this the right
way?" she asked.

That she could still be weighing up the options at this late
stage astounded me and it seemed best, therefore, that it was
me who was taking the initiative, as she had suggested, and

not her. Although she was one of Andy's group of friends I was involved in all this much more than she was. It was the first ladder I had gone up for a long time.

"You're not suggesting that we just walk away, are you?" I countered.

"Well, we could, couldn't we?"

"And forget about Andy?"

"It's Andy's business, John. He didn't ask you to do this," she reasoned.

"I'm not going to walk out on him, Karen."

"What happened wasn't your fault," she insisted. "You definitely don't belong in this kind of thing. Or do you. Am I missing something?" she asked irritably.

I was no stronger to not belonging. I didn't belong in Bartons sales office. My heart wasn't in it. I was a mere guest in what had once been my grandfather's house and I didn't really belong there either. And no matter how singularly impressed I had been by their beliefs I didn't belong in the Church in the way that the Pastor and Linda did.

"I practically gave the package away, Karen."

"He took the package off you at gun point, John."

"I should have seen him coming."

"He would have got it off you in some other way, somewhere else," she argued, sounding exasperated.

"Karen, it's you who doesn't have to do this, not me."

"Well we'd better walk the rest of the way," she said, ignoring my comment.

"Walk?"

"We can't just drive in through the front gate, can we?" she said impatiently, opening the car door.

I followed her across the road walking along the grass verge with her for about fifty yards or so, until she turned off and led me through an open gate into an uncultivated field.

"You can see the back of the Caravan Park from over there," she told me, pointing on ahead of us.

Although it was getting dark, I could make out how neat her shoulders looked beneath her cardigan, and how her narrow waistline enabled her to walk with poise over the broken ground. She was athletic, graceful, attractive, but that wasn't all. What was it about her? At last, when we had reached the barbed wire fence separating us from the field that lay adjacent to the Park, we stood behind a clump of bushes for a while, and looked up and down the row of caravans.

"It's the fifth one down from the left," she said, in a whisper. "So what do we do now?"

"You don't do anything, Karen. You go back to the car."

"Don't start that again," she snapped.

"Well, we can't just walk across the field, can we," I told her. "They could see us, even in this light."

"They're definitely there. I can see the car," she cut in.

There were a variety of bushes and trees skirting the field and I realised that it might be possible, after all, for us to get quite close without being seen. There was no sign of life coming from any of the other caravans and no other cars in the immediate vicinity, either.

"We'll skirt round the edge of the field and come up from the far end," I said to her in a commanding tone of voice, although still fully aware of the odds that were stacked up against us.

When we had come to within ten yards or so of the caravan we crouched down behind some bushes again. She looked at me questioningly. For a moment, which seemed frozen in time, I felt there was definitely something in our relationship that was being strengthened by this situation and was becoming more obvious, but which hadn't been created by it.

I took the gun from my jacket pocket, surprised at how comfortable it felt in my hand, and released the safety catch. It was too late to think about recoil or calibre, although I felt the weapon suited me.

As I peered through the bushes I could hear, against the silence, faint movement from inside the caravan and could just make out a shadowy figure brush against the curtain on the rear window.

"Now what," Karen whispered.

"Well, we can't just wait here until they come out, can we?"

"But you don't know for certain that there are only two of them, John," she said, turning her gaze away from the caravan to look anxiously into my eyes. "You can't just burst in on them, if that's what you mean."

She was right. But how long could we remain here, crouched down behind the bushes like two peeping toms?

chapter
nineteen

As I pictured the occupants, sheltered and warm inside, while we crouched outside in the cold, I thought of something that might get things moving.

Creeping up to the caravan and crawling down the side I reached the Calor gas cylinder that lay beside it, confident that no-one had heard me. Disconnecting the hose, I twisted the bracket out of shape, and crawled back to rejoin Karen in the bushes.

Someone came out, almost at once.

"It's worked," Karen whispered.

It wasn't enough, though. Who was still in the caravan? I wondered. But my work on the 'bracket' had helped, I saw. A second man appeared. It was Steve, who joined his companion bending over the cylinder. Although there might still be someone else inside, whatever it was I was going to do, I felt I had to do it right then!

With the gun gripped firmly in my hand, I came to within

a few feet of them before they heard me. They both looked round, still on their haunches, then stood up to face me.

"Who's still in there?" I asked them, nodding towards the door.

"Nobody," one of the men answered. It was the man who had taken the package from me in the lay-by and the same smile that he had worn on his face then was beginning to flicker on his lips.

"Where's the package?" I demanded of him.

"We don't have it," he said peevishly.

"Where's the package?" I repeated, moving closer to them. "If you don't tell me I'm going to drop one of you," I said coldly, using one of Andy's expressions as if it was my own.

"Look, can't we come to some kind of arrangement about all this, John?" Steve said in a surprising, conciliatory tone of voice.

"For the last time, give me the package!" I said, levelling the gun at him.

"It's inside," the smiling man said.

"Where?"

"I'll show you," he answered, turning towards the door.

"You won't," I snapped. "Just tell me where it is."

"It's in a cupboard in the bedroom."

This wasn't a job for one person, I realised, greatly relieved to see that Karen had joined me of her own accord.

"I'll look," she said, going towards the door, while the two men stood there, motionless, staring awkwardly at me, and then at Karen as she went into the caravan.

Steve, even more so than the smiling man, looked dangerous. I knew what he would be thinking. To him, it wouldn't seem likely that I would pull the trigger. He knew I was only a salesman in Bartons. I wasn't really one of Andy's group, not like Big Tom. But I also knew that he wouldn't be certain, and I stared at him threateningly to reinforce his doubts.

"Is this it?" Karen asked, as she re-appeared in the doorway gripping the package tightly in both hands.

"That's it," I shouted back. I could see where it had been torn open by the smiling man when he had examined its contents in the lay-by.

As she came over, there was an instant in which I saw, too late, that she was entering the field of fire and was passing between me and the two men. At almost the same time I knew I should have squeezed the trigger and stopped Steve taking advantage of what she had done. Instead, I hesitated.

Steve sprang at me, the weight of his body causing me to stagger back off balance. Although I absorbed the first few blows he rained on me quite well, I knew I wouldn't last for long. I was up against a determined and ruthless opponent, and, in spite of the many successful punches I had delivered in my youth, and lacking the killer instinct, what chance did I really have? But I still knew a few basics and managed to break free, pushing out the clenched fist of my left hand in an attempt to hold him off. I had done this often, years ago, and knew that it didn't always work. But I also knew that it usually made your opponent hesitate, and he did.

As he renewed his attack I couldn't believe my luck. He was holding my other arm and clenched fist in disdain in his efforts to get closer. It was coming back to me. I was keeping my large bony hand straight at the wrist and was prepared to punch from the shoulder. This fight maybe wasn't all that different after all, I saw to my surprise, for he was actually leaving his face exposed as he moved in on me. It was probably the only chance I was going to get and I knew I couldn't afford to be even slightly off balance. I came round, just in time, and the heavy right-handed punch that

I managed to deliver carried with it all the strength that was in me. When I felt the blow land on his jaw I knew it would stop him.

As I stood watching its effect I knew that nobody had taught me how to punch like this. Were my Aunt Grace's fears not so far fetched after all? Was it in my genes? But it had been a lucky punch, too, I knew, so maybe it was all down to chance. The result was the same, however, Steve staggered back and slumped down onto his knees.

"The gun, John," I heard Karen shout, as I turned to see her grappling with the smiling man in what had obviously been an attempt by her to keep him from interfering in the fight. He had a grip of both of her wrists and was overpowering her. Angrily hurling her up against the side of the caravan he rushed at me as I made my way towards the weapon where it had fallen on the grass. I took the full weight of his body crashing into me and at the same time the glancing blows he at once managed to land on me. As I staggered back one of his punches landed on my shoulder and drove me back onto the step outside the open door of the caravan. He came towards me again and sensing he was going to get the better of me I backed up the steps and stood in the doorway in the hope of fending him off. He came up after me and I kicked out at him just in time.

When he came at me again the jet from the very aptly named multi-purpose dry powder extinguisher, which I had snatched from the wall just inside the doorway, hit him full in the face.

He clattered back down the steps, coughing, rubbing his eyes and waving his arms about, helpless, as I threw the empty, but surprisingly heavy extinguisher at him. The metal casing caught him on the shoulder and I wondered what was coming next.

Beyond the suffocating cloud of dry powder I saw him get to his feet and make for the weapon. He reached it before I did but, as he clumsily struggled to pick it up, rubbing his eyes, I took a running kick at it and watched it slide away from him on the grass.

He raced after it but came to a sudden halt as Karen beat him to it, picking up the gun and pointing it at him, holding it clumsily in both hands. She didn't look the part, but I knew what he would be thinking. He might get shot, even by accident.

As he was joined by Steve, who had risen shakily to his feet, his eyes screwed up too, with tears running down his cheeks, I knew the effect of the powder, which was an irritant and not a poison, would soon wear off. But not too soon, I hoped.

"You'd better take this, John," Karen said, handing me the weapon and going over to get the package.

"You win, John," Steve said resignedly. "No hard feelings."

"Now what?" Karen asked, almost in a whisper, as she rejoined me.

"Nobody's really got hurt," Steve remonstrated with me. "Can't we just call it a day?"

"What do you mean nobody's got hurt? You shot Andy, didn't you?"

They stood there, both men, the fight having gone out of them, their eyes continually coming to rest on the gun.

"I didn't want that to happen," Steve said. "But you know what Andy's like. I tried to make him see sense. But I knew he was going to come after me and it was the only way I could stop him."

"By shooting him, you mean."

"I tried to shoot him in the foot."

The scene was halfway into a gangster movie and I was

acting my part quite well, almost believing it myself. But it had to end in the real world.

I hadn't the patience to tie them up and I didn't have the time either, for people were beginning to appear outside some of the neighbouring caravans.

In the real world, I wasn't going to finish this the way I should have. I wasn't going to shoot anyone. I couldn't bring myself to go as far as that, not quite. Was I, after all, neither one thing nor the other and was the human race that way too, neither essentially good nor essentially bad? That I was still determined to be a player of some sort seemed to answer my question.

"If I let you go, how do I know you won't come after us?" I asked him, looking at the smiling man, too.

"It's all gone wrong for us now," Steve said. "We took our chances, and it hasn't worked out for us."

"The whole business is too messy," the smiling man agreed. "All we want to do now is to put in some mileage, which is what we should have done in the first place," he said, glancing at Steve.

They looked as though they meant it. It sounded right. But I believed them mainly because I wanted to believe them. We had to get away.

With Karen by my side clutching the package, we moved back from them towards the bushes. They made no attempt to follow and, as we crouched down in the same position we had taken up when we had first arrived, we watched them get into their car and drive off.

It seemed that we were almost home and dry. But I wasn't certain. This was the big league I was in. Was I considering all the angles?

I looked at Karen as she once more settled in the car beside me. How I felt about her wasn't clear. Although she belonged to Andy there was a sense in which she seemed to belong to me, too. How much closer could you get to someone after all this?

Her cardigan was crumpled, with a button missing at the top, and a strand of hair was hanging down over her eye, but her dangerous and demanding encounter with these men had left her looking every bit as attractive, although in an entirely different way. How many ways were there?, I had to ask myself.

Sure now that we weren't being followed, I began to look forward to seeing Andy. What had happened showed I was no longer at the bottom of the learning curve, struggling to survive in Andy's world. I had made my mark.

We sat in silence for most of the journey. I felt relieved and satisfied, and for a while gave little thought to the overall situation. The Operation, Steve, and the smiling man were all still out there somewhere. But surely, as soon as we got back, Andy would know what to do.

As we reached his caravan Karen handed me the package. This was what I had wanted her to do. I was the one who had lost the package and I wanted it to be clear to Andy that I was the one who had got it back.

But I wasn't pleased that she might be aware of this, and not just because she had played as big a part in it as I had. Maybe I did want a pat on the back from Andy, but what she might think of all this felt more important. Having gone up in her estimation, I wanted to stay there.

I had managed to get the package back. I could do what criminals were inclined to do. I could survive in this world, even if I didn't belong in it. I had shown Karen that I was up to it and I was looking forward to letting Andy know I was, too.

But I wasn't that far gone. Deep down I knew I was thinking like the salesman whose sale had dropped into his lap, although in this case I had been throwing rather than selling an extinguisher. And it might not even have gone off. Like a second-rate salesman I was trying to take the credit for my good luck.

If I hadn't laid the package down on the passenger seat at that point, so that she could take charge of it, I felt I would have deserved what happened next.

"Andy's not here," she shouted from the door of the caravan. "And he's left his crutch behind."

chapter
twenty

ANDY COULDN'T HAVE WALKED VERY FAR WITHOUT a crutch, and his car was still there. He might still turn up, we hoped.

Meanwhile, we drove slowly round the Park several times, and looked on the beach, too. Eventually Karen made some tea and we hung about for a good while longer.

Much later, in the Old Toll Bar, we stayed until closing time, still hoping that Andy might hobble in, apologising for not letting us know where he had gone. But he didn't, and eventually, we had to assume that it hadn't taken the Operation long to find out that the package had gone astray. And it wouldn't take them long to find out about us either, I realised anxiously. When we left, having invited her back to the flat, I drove off quickly, anxious to leave the unlit corners of the car park behind. The package was lying at her feet, as if it was a time bomb, except for the banknotes that were protruding from the tear made in it by the smiling man.

As we went into the flat I felt something akin to a sense of occasion. This was where I nursed my disappointments, got transported by Chopin, and renewed my strength. Karen was crossing more than one threshold.

I had everything I needed here. I could shut myself away for days. The freezer was full. The location was secluded. I had a sanctuary.

But not now. As Andy had put it, I was a target. How long would it be before some faceless person from the Operation came knocking on the door?

"This is a nice place you've got here,." Karen said, as she settled across from me on the sofa. "Is that an original painting?" she asked, noticing the picture propped up on a chair in the corner.

"You like it?"

"I do," she answered, going over to take a closer look.

"It looks better from a distance," I advised her.

"John Grant," she read out. "Is he a relative?" she asked coyly.

"He is," I said, pleased at the effect this would have on my image.

"Art was my favourite subject at school," she then told me. "I must have taken a wrong turning somewhere."

"You too?"

"How do you mean?"

"Would you like some beans on toast?" I asked, to avoid going into the matter of my precarious pathway through life, but also to take my mind off the effect she was having on me. There was nothing I could do about this, I had to keep reminding myself. But if she hadn't been Andy's girl would I have stood a chance with her anyway? I knew I had to stop thinking about her in this way. What good could it possibly do!

"Beans on toast," she exclaimed, her face lighting up. "Where's the kitchen?"

As we lingered over the meal, I felt as if I was sitting in an expensive restaurant. The same crumpled cardigan fitted her very well at the shoulder and the button missing at the top had become an adornment. With someone like her it wasn't clothes that made the woman.

Her attitude towards me was completely different now, but since she was, in a sense, a captive audience and might feel obliged to be as nice to me as she was being, I knew I couldn't make too much of it.

We ate in silence for a while. But again, as it had been at the dance in the caravan park, it wasn't an awkward silence. It definitely wasn't, even if she did have plenty of other things on her mind, just like I had. What on earth were we going to do next, for instance?

"And your job at the Casino, have you been there for long?" I asked her. It wasn't small talk. Everything about her interested me but I had another reason for asking, too.

"Four or five years."

"Good people to work for?"

"The best employer I've ever had."

"How well do you know them? I mean could you ask them to put us in touch with the Operation?"

"John, I'm only an employee, she protested. I'm in Personnel and Accounts most of the time. It's not much different from any other job."

"So it's not a good idea."

"I suppose I could always ask."

So she wasn't involved with the Operation, at least not in the way that Andy was. I knew that for certain now. But her mood had changed, and that seemed just as important right then.

"Will I put on some music?" I asked her, going over to the drawer and thumbing through the CDs.

"What do you have?"

"Chopin, mainly."

"Who?" she asked.

"World class piano music."

"Really?"

But I knew she didn't mean it. Karen wouldn't be short on general knowledge, and everyone knew who Chopin was.

"I don't suppose he'll be your cup of tea," I said awkwardly trying not to sound patronising.

"Too sloppy," she said, screwing up her face.

I fell for it.

"Don't worry, I told her, I can listen to ordinary music too. But what makes you think he's sloppy", I asked. "He's anything but that."

"Only kidding," she said. Of course I would like to hear some Chopin."

"He's not just a collection of pretty tunes, you know." I pointed out, still hoping to save face and justify my taste in music.

Slipping the CD into place I pressed the button and sat back in my chair, exactly as I had done so many times before. But I didn't want to be transported to that other world of being, not right now. The music was for her. With her legs crossed, she began to rock her suspended foot in time with the waltz and her ankle and leg, swinging rhythmically in support, were soon competing with the music for my attention. For a while, Chopin faded into the background.

When I changed to the Nocturnes, however, Karen and the music converged. What she did to me and what Chopin did to me were clearly related. But having them with me in the same room must have effected my judgement for what was I doing thinking about her in this way, yet again? It wasn't Karen and Chopin that belonged together, it was Karen and Andy. Karen was Andy's girl, not mine.

But I couldn't help thinking that the Nocturne in C Minor had been written with a situation like this in mind. The music was beginning to 'beam me up', in spite of myself, indicating perhaps that Chopin had once experienced something similar to what I was going through with Karen. I wondered what he had done about it. If only I could learn something from him, in this higher world of knowledge or being that he took you to.

*

She came through from the bedroom wearing the dressing gown I had given her the night before. It certainly looked better on her than it did on me, probably for any one of a number of different reasons that were rattling about in my head.

"Just what I needed," she said, as she watched me pour some cornflakes onto her plate.

"Did you sleep?"

"The bed was fine."

I tried to ignore the appeal of the unruly strands of auburn hair that brushed her shoulders. I knew I had to keep my thoughts focused on the idea that had come to me during the sleepless night I had spent on the sofa.

The immediate danger was less than I thought. I could see that quite clearly now. Until the Operation actually got the Package back it was unlikely they would attack us with wilful abandon.

I had got things the wrong way round. I shouldn't be running away from these people, I should be trying to get in touch with them. They wanted the package, and I wanted to give it to them, albeit in exchange for Andy, and in the hope that they would leave us alone.

"We'll have to handle this one step at a time," I said to her, reluctantly trying to put my feelings for her to one side.

But she was looking at me wide eyed, as she had done when we had crouched down behind the bushes outside the caravan. Seeing that side of her again almost overwhelmed me.

"They want the package, and we want Andy," I stated, as solemnly as I could.

"Right."

"So we give them the package."

"Give it to whom, exactly?"

"The Operation."

"I know that. But how?"

"Instead of waiting on them to come to us, we go to them," I told her.

"So you've decided you want me to speak to someone at the Casino, after all?"

"I can't think of anything else."

As she went to get dressed, I settled in my usual chair and looked about the room. Only a few days ago I had dreaded losing this place. Now it seemed no more than a staging post, one that I would willingly leave behind if only I could leave my present set of circumstances behind with it.

I reached for a CD but decided against it. Chopin could relate to an event that was in the past, or one that I hoped might occur in the future. He seldom pushed me into taking action, or enlightened me as to the best course I should take, right now, which was what I needed.

But I had to think all this through, I told myself warily. Was asking her to go to the Casino really such a good idea? Hadn't she done enough already? What was I thinking of, putting her at risk again in this way?

"Forget it, Karen," I said, as she came back into the room.

"You don't want me to go, after all?" she enquired.

"No."

"So what do we do instead?" she asked.

The two ideas hadn't come to me at the same time. I knew in my heart which one had come first, and I was glad about it. I had to get her to a safe place. But I had to get the package to a safe place, too. Although it had got us into all this trouble it could also, if used as a pawn to bargain with, be the means of getting us out of it.

"Do you have anywhere you could go to get away from all this? I asked her.

"Where we could hide out?"

"Where you could hide out, with the package?"

"And leave you here by yourself, you mean?"

"They could burst in here at any time and take it off us, Karen," I pointed out impatiently. If that happens what do we do about Andy then, assuming we're still in one piece?"

"You don't think they'll let him go? I mean as soon as they get the package?" she asked.

"Karen, I don't know the answer to that. But as long as they don't have the package he should be all right. I'm almost sure of it."

Later, we walked down a long country lane into a neighbouring estate. As on the first run, on the pathway leading to the canal embankment, I felt confident that no unseen person was following us, although I took more than an occasional look over my shoulder just to make sure.

"Phone me later this evening," I told her, giving her my number as she boarded the bus. "Don't say where you are, unless I specifically ask you to," I warned her.

I felt a sense of relief that she would soon be out of danger but it saddened me to think that there wasn't going to be a completely happy ending to this part of it. Not the ending that I wanted. Karen wasn't going to be a permanent feature in my life.

But hadn't I known this all along? Why was there now a sense of loss attached to it? How could I lose her when she had never belonged to me in the first place?

She turned, unexpectedly, and stepped back down from the platform to embrace me in what I reluctantly felt was no more than an affectionate farewell hug. As her thighs pressed against mine they felt like objects of worship. Was this as close as I was ever going to get to her?

I had no idea where she was going but if the Operation caught up with me it wouldn't do them any good. I wouldn't have the package. I wouldn't even know where it was. If they wanted it, they were only going to get it when Andy was safe.

But how long was I going to have to wait for something to happen?

The Operation hadn't taken long to come on the scene once the package had gone astray. Only a short period of time had elapsed since the smiling man had held me up in the lay-by and Andy had disappeared from the caravan.

But did it make any difference? Sooner or later they were going to find me. I would just have to sit about in the flat indefinitely until they turned up.

But as I thought of the protracted mental and emotional torment involved in hanging about like this I decided instead to head for the office. I had to find something to occupy my mind. They could just as easily catch up with me there anyway.

chapter
twenty-one

OH HOW I ENVIED BENNY AS I SAW HIM SITTING there at his desk trying to look and sound like a 'real' salesman. Up until I had lost the package most of my worries hadn't been all that different in kind from the ones that he would be dealing with right now. His mind would be occupied with thoughts about where his next sale was coming from and how he could avoid getting on the wrong side of Sears.

Of all people, I knew exactly how he felt. Although the word that best described his circumstances was seldom used nowadays, Benny was in bondage, almost a kind of modern day Hebrew slave. And I wasn't being facetious, for Sears could deprive him of the only means he had of paying his mortgage, upon which rested so much. But in the light of what I myself was going through now I wished I could change places with him. Losing your job was bad but it wasn't lift-threatening. Neither was meeting with total failure in the attempt to close a sale. All of these paled into insignificance as I again weighed up the facts surrounding the disaster which had befallen me. The thought of being put out of my house, as Benny's fellow Jews in Europe had once been, no longer seemed so bad. But I had moved to the next stage, which for them had been deadly, and I felt almost as bad as they must have done. I was being hunted down.

Reading somewhere in the book Collection about the various natural disasters which had occurred in the last hundred years or so, in which a million people had been killed by storms, over nine million by floods, and even more by drought and disease hadn't effected me all that much. They hadn't made me sick to the teeth, like I was now. Even when the Pastor had cleverly drawn comparisons between some of these comparatively recent events and similar events in history and given reasons for them, convincingly coloured by his view of things, of course, my response had been more intellectual than emotional – the breaking of the moral law was a crime, and crime didn't pay. But now that I myself was directly involved, being hunted down, just like those unfortunates in that great man-made disaster which had befallen the Jews, my response was quite different. The effect on merely one victim, myself, meant more to me than the effect on millions. It had very nearly brought me to my knees.

Like the great British statesman, Winston Churchill, who had said of himself in the Book Collection, concerning his escape, as a young man, from a Boer Prison Camp, 'I had nowhere to hide'. Confessing that he had harboured anti-religious feelings at that time and had turned to philosophy and reason, the great man had gone on to describe how he had found these to be of little use in his hour of need and had finally had to cry to God for help.

Couldn't I, in a certain sense, say that the disaster which had befallen me was even worse than his? Churchill had known all about his enemies whereas I really had no idea who I was up against, except to say that they posed a serious threat to my life. My enemy was someone I wouldn't recognise, or even fully understand. He could come at me from any direction and at any time. And even if I did see him coming would I, in the long term, ever be able to shake him off?

The element of surprise that had been mine at the caravan, when confronting Steve and the smiling man, was gone. I was a target now, a sitting duck.

I was almost at my wits end, reduced to that very state the Pastor had described as so often as being necessary to make men realise their frailty and powerlessness, to show them where they really stood in the grand order of things even if, in my case, it hadn't taken a flood or an earthquake to do it.

With thoughts like these running through my head, I was beginning to think that I had been wrong in coming to the office. It might have been better, after all, if I had stayed in the flat and listened to some Chopin, even if it wouldn't have done much good. But what about that other art form? which was hanging there, right next to me, on the wall. Maybe the picture would help to take my mind off things, as it had done so often in the past.

It worked, but not in the way that I wanted. The fact that the girl in the picture was no longer Linda, but Karen, unsettled me even more. Try as I might, I couldn't restore Linda to where I thought she belonged. When I ended up imagining myself sitting on the grass watching the ducks I knew the out-of-the body experience that Beethoven associated with music, the same one that I had just then been hoping to gain from the picture, had become mere day-dreaming. I would have to settle for this.

As I gazed aimlessly out of the window noticing a vehicle drawing into the car park, I realised I couldn't afford to lapse into this state of mind. I had to keep my wits about me. The occupants of this car would have to be scrutinised as they got out, regardless of the fact that I didn't even know what kind of people the Operation would send. I couldn't expect everyone who worked for them to look like Andy or Big Tom. Would they be inclined to look something like Steve or the smiling man? They might as well be invisible, for all the difference their appearance was going to make to me, I concluded fatalistically.

But surely, I asked myself once more, the Operation wouldn't harm me as long as they thought I had the package? Hadn't I already made up my mind about this? On the other hand was it expecting too much to think that they would reason with me, treat me almost as an equal, want to bargain with me? Wouldn't they be more inclined to be rough on me right from the start to get me to tell them where the package was?

But I didn't know where it was. If they wanted it they were going to have to negotiate with me, I persuaded myself one more.

"Do you know these people?" I asked Benny, pointing out the window at the occupants alighting from the car.

"They were here last year."

How different Benny's circumstances were from mine, I thought again, as we studied the two men who were walking towards the entrance.

It didn't matter to him who these men were. He could look out the window with nothing much more than the weather on his mind.

Another car was coming in. Benny didn't even bother to look up. I couldn't take my eyes off it.

Waiting about like this in the office, instead of in the flat, definitely wasn't working, I could see. How could it, when I had something like this hanging over my head? What was I thinking of? It was a bit like being a condemned man patiently waiting on the firing squad to arrive, although not quite, for I still had a way of escape, I told myself. I could get into my car and drive off. There was still time. But drive where? And what about Andy? And what about Karen?

"You were supposed to hand in your paperwork," Benny whispered across to me as if someone could hear us though the wall. "Sears was asking where you were."

I was guilty of both of the charges that I guessed were about to be levelled against me by my boss – two mere pin pricks that would once have seemed serious threats to my wellbeing. I was a latecomer, and I had forgotten to hand in some work sheets.

"Let him wait," I said to Benny, relishing the startled look he gave me. "Who does Sears think he is?" Hadn't much more important people than him had to wait, I asked myself. Hadn't I read in the Book Collection of the two famous American Generals, George Marshal and Hap Arnold, commanding between them about eleven million men, who had had to hang about for forty minutes on the unsheltered platform of a remote British railway station, looking impatiently at their watches, because their train was late? It felt good to be able to downgrade my relationship with my boss in this way. Sears was no longer playing such a crucial part in my life.

But reflecting on how Chopin hadn't helped me and the picture on the sales office wall hadn't either, I saw now that this excerpt from the Book Collection fell short too. I couldn't really afford to treat Sears with the contempt he deserved. I would still have to pay lip service at least to the fact that, in this place, he was still the Boss.

And so, not just music and art, but history, too, seemed to be of most use 'after the event', or 'before the event', I reflect wanly, not when you were right in the middle of it. But if thoughts such as these could bob about in my head at a time like this then maybe the apprehension, anxiety and fear of the last few days was beginning to get to me. That this situation couldn't go on for very much longer, was becoming all too obvious.

chapter
twenty-two

I NEVERTHELESS FELT ALMOST RELIEVED WHEN Sears sent for me, although his particular brand of unpleasantness would only be a distraction on this occasion. But it would keep my mind occupied. I was probably about to be reprimanded for failing to hand in my paperwork and possibly for being late, too. Did I care, because he was still the boss? Not a bit of it, right then. I was actually looking forward to it.

"I believe you've got something that belongs to me," Sears stated, as soon as I had taken my seat.

I laid the paperwork on his desk, prepared and unworried. He couldn't hand me down a death sentence and he wasn't going to offer me a rise. Whatever it was he had in mind for me didn't really matter any more.

"Oh yes, the paperwork," he said, taking up the sheets without looking at them and laying them aside. Had I wrong-footed him by not apologising at once for my misdemeanours,

I wondered, or was he going to deal with my bad timekeeping first? He didn't look particularly annoyed, I noticed uneasily. Instead, he was staring at me thoughtfully, rather than aggressively, which I knew was uncharacteristic of him when he was about to deliver a reprimand.

"Do you want me to do some more cold calling, Mr Sears?" I asked politely, feeling that I had to say something, anything.

"Oh yes, cold calling," he replied ponderously.

Throwing his pencil onto the desk he sat back in his chair and smiled at me. It didn't look like he was going to be too hard on me, after all. He was probably going to tell me that my sales figures weren't good enough, or perhaps, merely elaborate on my shortcomings in general. Or did he really have something much worse in mind, I thought, with feigned apprehension – was he intending to take me by surprise?

"Can we start again," he said.

Surprised that paperwork and cold calling didn't seem to be on his immediate agenda and that his approach seemed to be conciliatory rather than confrontational, I wondered what kind of dirty trick he might be about to try and play on me.

"I believe you've got something that belongs to me," he said, in a casual tone of voice, completing disarming me.

"You mean the paperwork, Mr Sears?"

"Hardly," he answered, unsettling me even further.

I was at a loss as to what he wanted. And annoyed too that he was still capable of getting under my skin like this. He certainly knew how to do that for, even yet, I had no idea what was on his mind. I at least knew that there was nothing he could throw at me that would be nearly as bad as the trouble I was in with the Operation but I still wanted to know what he was getting at, even if only to silently pour scorn on it.

"The Package," he said. "I want the Package."

I could hardly believe what he had just said. That I could have been so completely unaware that he was in any way connected to my present problems was bad. How many other things was I missing?

"I know you have it," he added. "I had a phone call from Steve."

Here it was again. I had made another fundamental mistake. The smiling man had come up on me in the lay-by and caught me unawares and, in spite of this, and my growing awareness of such threats, Sears had now done much the same thing. I just hadn't seen him coming!

But this was a different world from the one I was used to, I quickly reminded myself. I couldn't be expected to know everything. This was a world in which there were none of the usual rights and wrongs, a world in which I couldn't afford to waste time on self-recrimination. It didn't matter that it had never entered my head that Sears might be involved. It was how I handled it that counted.

"I don't have the Package," I said to him, just like the smiling man had said to me when I had confronted him outside the caravan.

Sears wasn't looking at me contemptuously, as he usually did when I told him something he didn't want to hear. I would still have to be careful, though. Even more careful.

"I know you have it," he repeated, in an impatient but polite tone of voice. "Steve phoned me, as I've already said. He was only too anxious to tell me about what had happened, that it was you who had the package and that it was you I should be going after, not him."

"Where's Andy?" I countered, beginning to feel I could adjust to this new set of circumstances. After all, I still had the package or, at least, Karen did.

"Andy's quite safe," he said. "Give me the package and I'll tell you where he is."

I wished I could take him at his word. But in this kind of thing I knew I couldn't take anything for granted. The idea of a straight swap, as Sears was suggesting, seemed too good to be true. It might have been what I had been hoping for all along but now that it seemed to be within reach I could see that it might not be the end of the matter. I couldn't be sure. Sears of all people was obviously involved in my plight. But in what way, or to what extent?

"I only want what's mine," he remonstrated. Surely it's not too much to ask."

He seemed to be a different person entirely from the one who had lorded it over me in my attempt to hold down the job and sell fire extinguishers. There was still no trace whatsoever of the usual harshness in his tone of voice, and his position on the right side of the desk no longer made him seem so overbearing.

In seeing the other side of him in this way had I just caught a glimpse of how he was able to hold on to the advantage life had given him over people like me? I wondered. I felt he wasn't just acting. He seemed to be sincere. But he would probably be equally at home with whatever impression he felt was the most appropriate one to further his interests at the time, I supposed. Getting what he wanted or what he needed, I felt, would seldom differ from what he thought was right. And he had almost convinced me, too. I wanted to believe what he was telling me, that we should cooperate with each other. He was making me sympathise with him, to want to trust him. And this, after all that I knew about him. I needed something out of the Book Collection to clear my head, but it wouldn't come.

Instead, 'Would some people never learn', I lamented to myself, my thoughts going off at a tangent. In fact, would men in general so often misjudge other men, often putting seriously flawed people into positions of power on the strength of their empty promises and outward appearance. Or letting vicious criminals go free because of their good behaviour in the controlled environment of the prison? Were people always going to be fooled by others so easily? Were men always going to be such atrociously bad judges of other men?

But at last, just in time, a passage from one of the books came to mind to shed some light on the matter. Hadn't Admiral Doenitz, appointed by Hitler as his political successor, a man of some ability whom even some of his adversaries on the Allied side had come to respect, been taken in by one of the greatest mass murderers of the Century? 'Hitler', the Grand Admiral had said when first captured at the end of World War II, 'was a man with an abundance of good heart, his mistake being, perhaps, that he was too noble, too loyal to colleagues, who had not deserved it.' Was Doenitz really stark raving mad in having had such an unusual opinion of such an unusual person? I asked myself. While the accuracy of his assessment of Hitler could rightly be called into question, the Grand Admiral's sanity had never been in doubt.

"What do you mean the Package belongs to you?" I asked Sears, now more than ever determined not to be taken in by him. Sears was a serious threat, someone who was capable of doing me immense harm, in spite of the great change that seemed to have come over him. I wasn't going to let my guard drop for an instant.

"The solution to all this is very simple," Sears said, ignoring my question.

"You think so?"

"Give me the Package and Andy will be released."

"You're speaking for the Operation, I take it?"

"The contents of the package belong to me, not to the Operation, Grant," he stated, once more taking me completely by surprise.

This was a hard fact to accept, I felt, astounded at what he had just told me. If there was some truth in it, how could I even be sure who it was I should be dealing with, or who it was I should have such good reason to fear.

"And what about the Operation, where do they fit in exactly?" I asked him, trying to see him as someone I could manipulate as he had once manipulated me, someone I could now face up to without having one hand tied behind my back. I had to feel like this. I could feel like this. It was me who had the Package, not him.

"The Operation won't be a problem," he replied. "You're not dealing with the Operation, you're dealing with me."

"So you say."

"You're not listening, Grant."

"I am listening."

"You're not. We both want the same thing as far as the Operation is concerned, don't we? We both want to have as little to do with them as possible. They're not the kind of people we want to get on the wrong side of, are they?"

I certainly couldn't disagree with him on this point. The prospect of meeting up with some of these invisible and deadly people definitely filled me with dread.

"Look Grant, I'm sure we can work this out. What would you say if I told you the Operation doesn't even know the package has gone astray?"

If he was speaking the truth, then I now knew even less than I thought I did about what was really happening.

"It's to do with the setting up of the new Casino, Grant," Sears went on to explain. "The package does really belong to me. It's the money I was paid by the Operation for certain help I was able to give them. As far as they are concerned I've been paid in full. They don't know anything about what has happened to the package. They know absolutely nothing about all this."

"Nothing about Steve or Andy, you mean?"

"Absolutely nothing. And its best that it stays that way, isn't it?"

If I could believe what he was telling me, it was good news, indeed. I wasn't a target. The Operation wasn't interested in me, or in the package. I wasn't being stalked.

"And so it's just between you and me," I said to him. But there were still pieces missing, enough of them to make me hesitate. Could I really believe him, about any of this?

"And what about Steve and the other man?", I added.

"Steve once worked for Andy, but I didn't know that when I took him on. Andy didn't trust him. He wasn't happy when he found out."

"So Steve double-crossed you."

"How was I to know he would do something like this?, Sears pleaded. He was really only an engineer, as far as I was concerned."

"How did he get to know about the Package?"

"I used him to deliver messages and papers, that kind of thing, when I was setting things up with the Casino. There was a lot of coming and going and these people don't like talking on the phone. But I should have known better, I just couldn't have been careful enough. Andy was right about him. I don't want the Operation to blame me though."

"For what?"

"For everything. The whole mess. They know Steve worked for me."

"But you've just said he stole the money from you, not them."

"It's not just the money. It's the idea of any of this getting out. Can you guess what's involved in running a Casino these days, especially in this country. The whole thing has got to look clean from top to bottom."

I could see he was as scared of the Operation as I was. But he wanted his money. Sears was Sears, even in all this.

"We might have a deal," I told him.

"I never meant Andy any harm," he added convincingly.

"So how exactly did it all end up like this?"

"When my money didn't turn up on time I got a bit jumpy. I'm not exactly experienced in this kind of thing. I went out to the caravan to see him. You know how Andy is about using mobiles. When he told me what Steve had done I didn't know how to handle it. I knew he didn't approve of Steve but maybe they had settled their differences or something like that so I didn't know if I could believe him. I panicked. Andy was unarmed, and hobbling about on a crutch. But he's not been hurt in any way by me, I assure you, and he's not going to come to any harm where he is."

"So how do we arrange this?"

"I have a boat down in the Marina – The Firefly."

chapter
twenty-three

As I left Sears' office and headed for the nearest exit, I saw Benny's head protruding from the half-open door of the sales office. I guessed he must be wondering where I was going. In actual fact, he knew as much about my destination as I did myself at that point for I just wanted to get into the car and drive, to get behind the wheel, where I was in control, and had enough knowledge and skill to keep out of danger.

It worked for a while but, like my other more complex means of escape – music, art and the Book Collection, driving about aimlessly wasn't going to solve anything. I was glad when it was at last time to go to the flat and wait for Karen to phone me. Was it possible that this flat, this one-time haven, might become a haven again, now that I was no longer in any immediate danger from the Operation? I asked myself.

I had made a good job of furnishing and decorating the place, I pointlessly observed, as I tried unsuccessfully to concentrate my attention on the events which had just unfolded. It was the kind of place I could have brought Linda to without feeling at a disadvantage. I tried to picture what this would have been like and imagined her sitting across from me on the sofa as Karen had done, filling the room with her presence, while I admired her legs and impressed her with my ownership of an original oil painting that had my surname on it.

For a while I imagined they were both sitting there across from me, side by side, Karen's smile holding me in its spell, while the rays from Linda's smile spread throughout the whole room.

So different from each other in personality and background, they nevertheless had that one defining feature in common. In this, I couldn't say which of them was the more attractive, although I knew that there was a difference of some kind in the way that I felt about them. I was equally aware that the true nature of this disparity was very difficult to define.

In spite of their strongly contrasting backgrounds Karen seemed every bit as refined as Linda, and Linda seemed as strong and determined as Karen, a resemblance which I would once have thought unusual. But as Andy had once pointed out, people who worked in Casinos nowadays had to be as presentable as those who didn't.

While Linda was well set-up with a neat figure, and was almost but not quite sturdy looking, Karen's thin legs and almost athletic build were suggestive of the stamina I knew she possessed. They were both 'almost' something other than what they were but this very nearness, in them, was potent.

I had made progress with Linda. But the direction in which I had had to go, in my innermost thoughts, to do this had made me realise that I would have to adopt a lifestyle that was foreign to me if I was to take the relationship any further. The fact that I couldn't see her making a similar kind of sacrifice for me, surely said something significant about our relationship, I reasoned sadly.

I had made progress in my relationship with Karen, too, which was only natural, I felt, in view of what we had been through together. But while this should have been on an entirely different plane, because she was Andy's girl, comparing the two of them in the way that I was doing suggested otherwise. I now seemed to be faced with two problems of a not dissimilar kind. I didn't know what to do about Linda, and there was absolutely nothing I could do about Karen.

I sprang out of my chair at the sound of the telephone.

"Where are you?" I asked Karen, trying to keep the excitement out of my voice.

"Is it safe to say?"

"Yes, absolutely," I told her, in a tone of voice that hid my lack of composure.

"I've ended up at Liz's", she told me.

Although surprised, I wasn't too concerned to hear this for after all, no one was chasing us now. It didn't really matter where she was.

"Are you ok?" she asked me, in a soft, concerned tone of voice.

"Stay there, Karen, I'll be right over."

I wondered to what extent and in what way she cared. Her question and her manner of asking it could mean different things.

*

Having taken the package from her, as soon as I got there, "I've to take it to Sears tonight," I told her, as Liz went to make some tea.

"Sears?"

"The money's his."

"You mean Sears is mixed up in all this?" she gasped. "So what do you think about it all, now?" she asked, when I had come to the end of my explanation.

"I'll have to go along with him."

As she rose to help with the tea I could tell from the strained expression on her face that she didn't agree with my suggestion and I thought I knew why. It was leaving too much to chance. There was nothing to fall back on.

"Did you know Big Tom has been on the phone from down South?" Liz asked, as she filled my cup. "He's been trying to get in touch with Andy."

I looked uneasily at Karen., wondering how much she had told her friend. Would Liz have been able to tell Tom on the phone that something had gone seriously wrong up here?

"And is he coming back up?" I asked her.

"Tomorrow some time," she said, dashing my hopes that immediate help might be at hand.

"I haven't told Liz what this is all about," Karen quietly explained to me, reading my thoughts, while Liz was out of earshot in the kitchen.

"Look you two," Liz chided, an affectionate smile appearing on her face, "you know I'll do anything to help that I can. What's the problem. What's this all about?"

"This is something I don't want to get you involved in, Liz," Karen said to her friend. "I really shouldn't have come here."

"I know. You've already said that. But where else would you go?" Liz scolded. "I always go to you when I have a problem, don't I?"

"Not a problem like this. Its something I definitely don't want you to get mixed up in," Karen told her.

"Surely I'm involved already," Liz insisted, looking at me. "I was there when you met him."

"Met who?" I asked, puzzled.

"She means you," Karen said.

Liz looked puzzled too now and Karen seemed ill at ease. "Me?"

"I'd better leave you two alone," Liz said, clumsily lifting up the empty tea pot and going back into the kitchen.

"Liz thinks you and I are an item," Karen said pointedly.

"An item?" How on earth does she think that?"

"I couldn't tell her exactly why I was so worried about you and why I had to contact you, so she's jumped to conclusions, I suppose."

"But what about Andy?"

"What about him?"

"I mean you and Andy."

"What on earth has Andy got to do with you and I being an item?" she asked, sounding genuinely surprised.

I had got a lot of things wrong recently but, if her words meant what I thought they meant, this was going to be my crowning achievement? Was the relationship between Karen and Andy not what I had thought it was?

"So what's Andy to you?" I asked her bluntly.

"I've been Andy's point of contact at the Casino. I thought you knew that. I do work there, remember!", she said scathingly.

"And that's all?"

"What do you mean 'that's all'? It's not been easy seeing that the changeover goes smoothly. It's a great big job," she said, misunderstanding me.

Her words confirmed my suspicions, though. Once more a seemingly trivial gap in my knowledge had become a major failure in my overall comprehension. My ideas on where she stood with Andy, and possibly on where she stood with me, too, had been seriously wrong. I had been getting it wrong all the time.

But what kind of impression had a mistake of this kind been making on her? I wondered anxiously. "I wasn't talking about the Casino," I pointed out to her. "I didn't mean that."

"I f you didn't mean that, then what exactly did you mean?" she asked.

"Karen. I thought you and Andy were, you know …"

"You thought what? How …"

"Look. Have I been wrong?" I asked, impatiently cutting her off.

"Now I get it," she loudly exclaimed, smiling in astonishment. "John, I was beginning to wonder about you. Andy's a really good friend, that's all. One of my very best friends actually."

"Wonder in what way?" I asked, as if I didn't understand.

"Look," she said, her smile fading. "It's maybe not the best time to discuss this."

It felt like it was the best time but I knew she was right. We were still in very serious trouble. Nothing else had changed.

"About the package," she went on. "You're surely not just going to hand it over, are you? Not to someone like him."

"He says he'll let Andy go."

"He says! Sears says! John, don't hold your breath", she snapped.

Her words told me what I should, undoubtedly, have already realised, and I had no excuse, I told myself. Even at this late stage I was reverting to type. In spite of all that had happened I was still projecting my own sense of decency and fair-play onto someone else and expecting them to act in the same way. And this, even when Andy was being held prisoner and our very lives, in spite of what Sears had said, might still be in danger.

And her life too, if I didn't do something about it, I realised.

"Look Karen, I've got to clear my head. I'm going to the flat to get some fresh clothes," I lied. We'll decide what to do when I get back."

chapter
twenty-four

With an hour to spare before I went to meet Sears at the boat, I sat in the flat going over the whole thing again, trying to be as clear-headed and objective as possible. One thing, at least, was glaringly obvious. I always seemed to be on the wrong end of things, trying to get shopkeepers to buy fire extinguishers, trying to accommodate myself to the Pastor's way of looking at things, and even, in a sense, feeling I had to get Bethea to accept me for 'what I was', when 'who I was' should have been enough. I was like a British soldier in the trenches in the early days of the First World War, always having to go over the top in spite of what he knew he was walking into.

The fact that many of these victims of suicidal military resolve, that I had read about, would have added fifty years to their lives it they had seriously taken into account the fact it was immediate death and not ultimate victory through attrition that was to be their lot and, of course assuming that they had been able to do something about it, seemed worthy of note. Wasn't I doing something just as futile? I was 'going over the top' to meet Sears at his boat with as much real knowledge of what I was up against as these soldiers had, or even worse, like some conscientious objector who thought the enemy would be nice to him if he was nice to them. After all that had happened this didn't say much for me, I knew. Or was the fact that mankind in general projected a blurred image of itself something I could use as an excuse? After all, I was far from being the only one who couldn't make up his mind about whether man was essentially good or essentially bad.

That a violent criminal could love children and be loyal to his friends suggested that man could often be a volatile mixture. As did the unusual fact that to his presentable young secretary, Gertrud Junge, Hitler had fbeen a kindly older man and one of the best bosses she had ever had.

But I couldn't afford to behave as if this mixture was going to settle in my favour and expect that Sears, a man I had no reason to think I could trust, would do as he said he would. There was too much at stake. This world had people in it who, from the very core of their being, could see little real or essential difference between right and wrong. I had to get it into my head, once and for all, that there were men like Eichmann out there, the Austrian Nazi who had sought out and relentlessly gathered together millions of Jews so that they might thereafter be murdered, whilst claiming at his trial in 1961 that he had had no personal antipathy towards them. And people like Rudolph Hoess, the Commandant of the extermination camp at Auschwitz, during whose tenure at least 1.5 million inmates were murdered, who actually felt himself to be a victim of the system, a man whose deepest regret was, when looking back over his 'career' that he hadn't been able to spend more time with his family.

Surely I could at last resolve this inner conflict about how I went about things. Surely with people like these men in the world, men who had a host of human characteristics in common with the rest of us, I couldn't let my guard drop for an instant, ever let someone have the edge on me. What the Pastor taught made a lot of sense but to even think along the lines of being 'as harmless as a dove' in a situation like this was ridiculous. The other part of the verse – being 'as wise as a serpent' had a better ring to it, although this wasn't enough either, I firmly concluded.

In going to meet Sears at his boat, therefore, I wasn't going to make another of these mistakes described in the Book Collection. The British Prime Minister, Chamberlain, I had read there, had assumed, prior to the outbreak of the Second World War, that Hitler was telling the truth about his desire for peace when he should have assumed that he wasn't. Chamberlain, it seemed, had preferred to believe that Hitler was a reasonable and honest man like himself simply because he could think of no other way of dealing with him if he wasn't. This could be me. But it wasn't going to be, not now.

Sears was an enemy, and I had to treat him as such. Imputing right motives to people like him in a situation like this didn't make sense, in spite of what the Pastor would seem to suggest. There was no way, I finally convinced myself, that you could deal realistically with the evil in men's hearts without sacrificing some of the purity in your own.

In the light of all this I could see that, right from the start, I would have to adopt a more realistic and, if needs be, unprincipled approach if I was meet Sears on his own terms. He simply couldn't be trusted, and if he had known some of the things that were running through my mind he would have felt the same way about me. I was prepared to do absolutely anything to make sure nothing went wrong and that Andy was safely released.

Did this mean, I asked myself warily, that there was no limit now to what I might stoop to in my new-found determination to deal with this matter realistically? Did it mean, for instance, that I could kill to achieve my ends? Was I to become just like some of the more worthy of these men in the Book Collection who had felt able to set aside the First Commandant to achieve their ends because they were fighting for a good cause. Was there nothing remaining of my old self that might separate me from them, nothing that might enable me to live with myself? Something that nevertheless might still give me an advantage!?

But what weapon other than the gun did I have? How else could I be sure of getting the better of Sears if my worst fears were confirmed and I found out I was being led into a trap? What else could I do but run the risk of taking a life, of becoming a murderer, for that was exactly what was on my mind?

But there was indeed another weapon, I began to see. It was one of Hitler's favourites, I knew, although a lot of good men had used it too. It wasn't as bad as setting aside the First Commandant so that you would be the 'fittest who survived'. I felt better already. The idea which was beginning to form in my mind wouldn't even call for the use of the gun. In fact, out of deference for what the Pastor taught, I wouldn't even take the weapon. I would stake all on the results of what I felt, all things considered, was the best way for someone like me to go about things. After all, I wasn't altogether unacquainted with the idea. Hadn't 'deceit', only recently, been one of the tools of my trade?

At the caravan with Karen, when confronting Steve and the smiling man, I had been carried along by events. The scene had already been set and the role I had had to play had been decided in advance. Although the scene I was now facing had likewise been set up beforehand the nature of my performance was going to be entirely different. I could see things quite clearly now, and the end was going to justify the means, too.

Sitting with the package on my knee I ran my fingers over the tear made in it by the smiling man. I remembered that when he had taken it from me in the lay-by, he hadn't actually counted the money. He had only checked to see that it was there. He had known who I was and what I was and hadn't seen the need to closely examine the contents.

There was every likelihood that Sears on this occasion wouldn't count the money right away either. At least not until I had formed some idea of what looked likely to happen next. I would, therefore, hold back some of it until I knew what I was up against, I decided. Or even until I felt sure that Andy and I were in the clear.

As I slit open the package on the kitchen table, I could see that the money consisted of one hundred-pound notes, laid out in four rows of five piles each. Each pile contained five wads held together by elastic bands. Taking one out and counting it, I found it to contain exactly £2,000. The package therefore held £200,000 in total.

What Sears had done to earn this money I could only guess. In the eyes of his paymaster perhaps a key vote, a bribe, or even a strong influence exerted on some important Planning Committee meetings would seem cheap at the price.

Squeezing fifty wads under the freezer, I laid out the remaining fifty on a fresh strip of brown paper and, in what later proved to be a crucial afterthought, removed the elastic bands.

When I had sealed it, I rubbed the new package on the kitchen floor a few times to take the newness off it, finally slipping it into a plastic carrier bag and taking it through to the lounge.

I was definitely thinking 'like' a criminal now. I could see that. But on this occasion I wasn't exactly thinking 'as' a criminal, I felt. For I was, in a sense, fighting for my life.

But was there anything I still hadn't thought of, I asked myself, something that I should be doing that I wasn't, something that would narrow the odds even further in my favour? I knew that there probably was but could, at the same time, see the futility of thinking about it now. Wouldn't Captain Smith on the Titanic, the great passenger liner that sank in 1912, have moved information on the icebergs, about which he had been warned by wireless messages, up his list of priorities, slowed his ship, even sat in the wireless room, if he had recognised their true significance at the time. Similarly wouldn't the British General, Lord Chelmsford, in command of the army invading Zululand in 1879 have given more personal attention to the defense of the Camp he was leaving behind at Isandhlwana where about eighteen hundred men had been slaughtered by Zulus armed mainly with spears of some kind.

What, therefore, should I be moving up my list of priorities as I went to meet Sears? What should I be paying more attention to? But since neither of these men, described so critically in the Book Collection, were hopeless incompetents I could at least see I had one thing in common with them. Like them I didn't have the benefit of hindsight and I would just have to do the very best I could.

Before any further anxiety could surface I saw that it was time to go.

chapter
twenty-five

As I stepped onto the deck of the boat, about to find out what I was really up against, it was a great comfort to know that on this occasion I had something which might work in my favour. I finally had an advantage. I was at last dealing with the world on its own terms and had unscrupulously narrowed the odds in my favour.

"Is Andy here?" I demanded of Sears as he came out of the cabin to meet me.

"I assume that's the package you've got there?," he asked.

"It is."

"Well, I'm afraid the answer to your question is, to be quite accurate, no, Andy's not here" Sears told me, abruptly.

That this was a bad start was all too obvious. Did he, too, have some hidden advantage? Did he perhaps have reason to think that if I didn't give him the package voluntarily he could just take it? I looked nervously about me, but we seemed to be alone.

"Don't worry Grant. It's just a precaution," he quickly explained. He's on another boat, that's all."

I felt I had to believe him. In view of what I had just done with the money, I couldn't really blame him for doing something like this. I would play this bit by ear.

The other boat was moored nearby and as we reached it, Sears stared pointedly back along the jetty.

"You're definitely alone?" he asked me, suspiciously.

I followed his gaze all too willingly. I thought I had seen movement down there too, and had been worried for the same reason that he had. But there was no one to be seen.

Opening the cabin door, he invited me to follow him inside where I at once saw Andy lying tied up on a bunk with some tape over his mouth.

"For God's sake, how long has he been like this? I exclaimed angrily, tugging at the tape with my free hand.

"Good to see you John," Andy gasped, a look of disbelief on his taught, unshaven features.

"That's far enough," Sears snapped at me. "Now can I have the package" he demanded.

It was a reasonable enough request, I knew, for it looked like Sears had kept his part of the bargain. So far, it was me who was doing the double crossing, not him.

I took the package out of the carrier bag and laid it on the table deciding, at that point, to keep it sealed until Andy was on his feet. But, at once, Sears began to tear frantically at the wrapping and the notes spewed out onto the table. Fortunately, without the elastic bands they formed the untidy heap that I had foreseen would make them difficult to count. Hoping the delay would give me enough time to complete my task I turned away again and struggled with the knots.

We all heard the noise, a kind of thump, and Sears looked at startled by it as I was. Someone else had come on board.

Quickly scooping up the pile of loose notes Sears stuffed them back into the carrier bag and went over to the cabin door.

"That noise, whatever it was, has nothing to do with me," I told him. "I have no idea who's out there."

I was losing precious seconds. I hadn't yet freed Andy and I wasn't sure of my next move. But the situation completely changed, yet again. A gun had appeared in Sears' hand.

"You go first, Grant," he ordered, pointing towards the door.

I wasn't sure what was on his mind but it was obvious he thought I was a part of this new problem, and that I was a possible solution, too.

"I'm coming out," he shouted from the doorway. "And Grant's coming with me."

Once more I had no idea what I was up against. Was this the Operation coming on the scene at the last minute, as I had feared, in spite of what Sears had led me to believe? Did it mean that if he didn't shoot me, they would? Was it as bad as that?

But Sears seemed every bit as uncertain as I was. It was obvious that this kind of thing wasn't in his field of expertise any more than it was in mine. Going up onto the deck in this way, to investigate, how could he know from which direction he was being threatened? He looked desperate.

As he pushed me out in front of him I expected the worst. I was on the wrong end of something again, and it wasn't just a desk.

Big Tom sent me sprawling, as he crashed down on top of us from the roof of the cabin. Still on my knees I turned in time to see Sears, from a similar position, get to his feet still holding the carrier bag, but without the gun.

As Tom lifted him up bodily and hurled him against the rail the carrier bag flew through the air disgorging some of the notes which fluttered about like streamers before landing scattered about beside the bag in the water.

Getting to his feet unsteadily, Sears stared over the side as if watching a loved one in distress. I could see what he was about to do. This was Sears. The greedy, heartless employer who had manipulated and oppressed me for so long. The man who only used people, who never treated them decently, who deprived his employees of their peace of mind and robbed them of their self respect. Was the moral law of God at last about to exact its demands? Was it true, as the Pastor had said, that whilst the ungodly may prosper, that bad people may meet with success, they only do so for a while? Like Himmler, the merciless Nazi mass murderer, and Goebbels the well-educated, unprincipled and evil Nazi propagandist out of the Book Collection, both of whom committed suicide when their day had come to an end, was Sears at last about to get what he deserved, I wondered, as I watched him jump overboard to retrieve the bag.

I could see that the air trapped inside it had caused it to swell up and stay afloat as the current carried it towards the harbour entrance. But gradually it lost its buoyancy, the notes spilling out into the water, and before Sears could reach it, it had sunk out of sight.

We watched Sears splash about in the water clutching some of the notes, as if trying to find the bag, and then, as if trying to keep afloat. None too soon, we saw he was in trouble and it took all of Big Tom's strength and agility in the water to reach him before he went under.

"Am I glad to see you," I told the big man, as Sears lay spluttering and coughing beside us on the deck, my voice unashamedly charged with relief and admiration.

Tom had just saved me from God knows what, and Sears from drowning, and yet his features had broken out into the broad, good-natured smile I knew so well from the pub. He seemed to be two different people. One – good natured, slow moving, and bulky. The other – deadly, quick, and powerfully built.

How on earth did you get here Tom?" I asked him, as I headed for the cabin to get Andy.

"From Liz's. I came back up when I realised something had gone wrong, when I couldn't get in touch with Andy. It was Karen who guessed you'd be down here."

As I untied Andy, explaining to him what had happened outside on the deck, I was surprised when he lay back on the bunk, shaking his head.

"John, you've got a talent for this kind of thing," he said, grinning.

"You mean Tom has."

"I mean I owe you one, John," he said, his grin fading. "Good to see you, big man," he said to Tom, as we joined him on the deck.

Sears was sitting there, soaked and dejected.

"So, what do we do now?" I said to Andy.

"You mean, with him?" he asked, poking Sears with a pole he had found lying on the cabin floor.

"We can't just leave him here, can we?" I reasoned anxiously.

"We don't do anything with him, Andy replied. It's up to the Operation. It's their money that's sunk to the bottom."

Sears looked up at us, a look of desperation on his face.

"Tell him, Grant," he begged.

"He says the money's his, Andy," I explained. "He says the Operation doesn't know anything about the package going astray."

"About Steve you mean."

"Steve worked for me, Andy," Sears pleaded. You know that. They know that. As far as they're concerned I've been paid what I was due. What good will it do telling them about Steve. They're not going to pay me twice, are they?"

I almost felt sorry for him as I watched him sitting there soaked to the skin, making no attempt to get to his feet. He had lost his money and very nearly his life. But 'oh how people like him squirmed when they were on the receiving end', I thought instead. Suddenly bereft of their power, no longer able to disregard the feelings of other people, oh how people like him then demonstrated the intimate knowledge they really had of what was right and what was wrong. And oh how much they wanted, actually expected, the reasonable and decent treatment they had so consistently and maliciously denied to others. Liars in their own hearts, denying the existence of the great moral laws concerning man's disposition towards others, and yet, when called to account, wholeheartedly invoking these very laws in their own defence. And so I didn't feel sorry for him. I was a judge who had been a victim.

"Why should we do you any favours," Andy said to him.

"Telling them won't do you any good, either," Sears pleaded in reply. "If the Operations thinks their cover is blown there's no saying what they will do to us.

"What will they do to you, you mean," Andy replied contradicting him, and then turning to Tom who stood shivering beside us. "What do you think, big man?" he asked

"I'll need to get out of these clothes, Andy," Tom said. "I suppose we could tip him over the side or something like that," he added helpfully.

Andy nodded slowly in agreement, but he was looking at me.

Tom followed his gaze and looked at me, too. They were going to let me decide.

The big man didn't look like a killer. Not a real killer. But he certainly looked like he was capable of being one if he thought it was necessary.

The outcome was hanging in the balance, therefore, and I could see that Sears realised this, too. The frightened, exhausted look had gone from his face. He now looked terror-stricken.

"Don't let them do this, Grant," he whined.

"We'd better get him out of sight in the meanwhile" Andy said to Tom, impatiently. "We'll take him into the cabin" and then, turning to me, again, "Come on John. Make up your mind. What do we do with him?", his words signifying to me that I was definitely one of them now.

*

As I watched them push and drag Sears into the cabin all I could think about at first was the money lying hidden back at the flat. At all costs I had to hang on to it. There was no point in saying to myself that, after all this, the money was no longer important. It was the other way round. After all this, money was more important than ever. I now knew of its power and that the lack of it was a kind of impotence. As far as I was concerned it was all going to hinge on this.

With Sears out of the way I would be sole owner of the bank notes tucked up under the freezer. He was all that stood between me and a clear-cut solution to all my problems.

And he had brought all this on himself. If he hadn't done what he had to Andy he wouldn't be in this situation. And if he hadn't so often treated me in the way that the had, I might have had some sympathy for him. But all he was to me now was unfinished business, a loose end.

This wouldn't be murder, it would be self-defence, I told myself, and I couldn't afford to let my guard drop now. In deciding to hold back the money I had fully engaged in this other way of life. I could now identify with Andy and could understand his attitude. It would be better if Sears got what he deserved. Better for all of us. And anyway, I wouldn't have to do anything myself. Big Tom would do it.

As I went over to the cabin to tell Andy of my decision I felt convinced I was doing the right thing. I was doing what any reasonable person would do in this kind of situation. True, not many people would advocate killing someone as a solution to their problems, not many decent people that is, but not many decent people would have been under the same kind of pressure as I had been under, and had been under for quite some considerable time.

All this apart, you certainly didn't have to squeeze people, ordinary people like me, very hard to bring out the worst in them, I reflected guiltily. Peer pressure alone could work wonders. What was so bad if everyone else was doing it, if your companions expected it of you, if Tom and Andy expected it of me? But hadn't that been one of the excuses put forward by the otherwise respectable working-class Germans described in the Book Collection, who had donned a uniform and set about slaughtering defenceless women and children?

Surely what I was going to do wasn't nearly as bad as that. Killing Sears wouldn't even turn my stomach, as their crime had turned theirs. Maybe I was more like Eichmann than I was like them. At his trial in Israel in 1961 for organising the mass murder of millions he had said that he had just wanted to be thorough, to do what had seemed to be the most efficient thing at the time. Like him, I didn't hate my victim and I wouldn't have to get my own hands dirty. Tom would do it for me.

I certainly wasn't deluded like Eichmann's superior Himmler, who almost eulogised bestiality during an address in which he called those who carried out his horrific orders decent men. Although perhaps I did resemble him in one way. I wanted to make sure, like he had, when he had incinerated the bodies of those he had shot or gassed, that I didn't leave any loose ends lying about.

That Andy and Tom were leaving this decision up to me meant a lot. I had finally arrived. I was entitled to bring a bit of my old self along and project these historical figures into the situation, however ludicrous and time consuming it might seem. And, anyway, I couldn't help myself. What mattered was whether or not these insights were leading me in the right direction. Who were these men I was so characteristically using to shed light on my predicament? Most of them had been on the wrong side. Was I being perversely selective?

But good men, too, like Field Marshal Haig in the First World War and Air Marshall Harris in the Second had gone down a not altogether dissimilar road. The former had repeatedly sacrificed the lives of his soldiers by conducting battles of attrition, while the latter, deeply convinced of the need for it, had dropped thousands of tons of high explosives on German cities killing thousands of unarmed and defenceless civilians. So it wasn't just the behaviour of evil men I was emulating, it was the behaviour of mankind in general.

At last I realised who the man was that stood at the apex of my current thought processes. I could see I was being driven in my attempts to justify killing Sears by the same forces that had driven Hitler. I was about to employ in effect the same evil means as he had, cold blooded murder, to achieve what I personally believed was a not ignoble end. Was it wrong of him to have wanted to gather his 'family' together, to unite them and restore their confidence; was it wrong of him to have desperately wanted more land so that they could fulfil themselves and get on in the world; to have tried to protect them from people he thought were a very bad influence, and from others who weren't good enough; and to have sought the very best and lasting solutions to his 'family's' troubles with their 'neighbours?'

That I was, just like him, carrying my thoughts to their logical conclusion, at last made me see the true nature of the company into which my Godless logic had taken me.

But did I really belong there? It certainly looked as though I did for, in my own small way, I was bending the rules to suit my needs, just like mankind in general did, and now, slowly but surely, I had reached the point where I was giving serious consideration to applying the ultimate sanction. Murder might not be in my heart, but it was certainly in my head.

"Come on John, say the word. Do we top him or do we not?" Andy shouted, his words from the real world crashing into my thought world. "We've got to get out of here."

I went over and looked into the cabin. Sears was lying tied up on the bunk, just as Andy had been a short while before.

"Don't let them do this, Grant," he whined. "What possible harm can I do you now?"

It wasn't that Sears posed much of a threat, I began to realise. It was more the idea of it. He was terrified of what we might do, and terrified of the Operation. And more importantly, from my point of view, he had no idea that I had kept back half of the money. The money was gone as far as he was concerned.

"Well, what's it to be, John?" Andy asked impatiently.

"I suppose he's taken a big enough loss already. What harm can he do us now," I said. "Look at him."

Andy's face was expressionless.

"Not much, I suppose" he agreed.

"Maybe we should just let him go," I suggested.

Was I being magnanimous in victory because of some of these men I had read of in the Book Collection and my aversion to their behaviour. Or was I trying to convince myself that, even under pressure, I would never behave like they had and try to utterly destroy my enemy, as most people sanctimoniously believe of themselves, until their own lives are threatened.

My very uncertainty, however, did say something. While evil might originate in the heart, as the Pastor said, the part played by the mind couldn't be left out. While we might shrink from doing certain things we could talk ourselves into anything, absolutely anything, even good people thinking it necessary to do evil in a good cause, and bad people to achieve their ambitions.

It was a great pity, therefore, that the people history shows us to be, the good as well as the bad, don't seem capable of self-improvement. If good people even yet could pass unwise laws and commit acts of great injustice then the solution certainly didn't lie in democratic government and legal niceties. Maybe Linda and the Pastor did, in actual fact, have the answer to all this, I felt really seriously, for the first time.

As Sears jumped onto the jetty looking ridiculous in his wet clothes, yet sufficiently recovered to hurry away as if he was trying to catch a bus, I felt euphoric as I took stock of the situation. He wasn't the only one who thought all of the money had floated out to sea. Everybody else did, too. No one but me knew of the 100 thousand pounds lying hidden under the freezer. No one.

chapter
twenty-six

THE DANGER HAD PASSED, ALL OF IT, BUT BEFORE I went to the party that was to take place at Liz's that night, I still had some important decisions to make. Going into the kitchen, I got down on my knees and pushed my hand under the freezer to get tangible proof of the fact that financial success, not failure, had become the key word in my life. I could now think about things from a position of strength. My problems, what remained of them, no longer seemed insurmountable.

Since no-one but me knew about the money, what exactly I should do with it didn't seem urgent and, of the several other matters competing for my attention, my thoughts on Linda and Karen soon re-gained the ascendancy.

The problem I had with Karen seemed to have unravelled itself in respect of the relationship I had thought she had with Andy, although I still had no idea where I really stood with her. The problem with Linda remained as it was. I couldn't separate her in my mind's eye from her enthusiasm for the Church and from the fact that she was Pastor Mackenzie's daughter. It seemed that, if I was to take things any further with her I would, at the very least, have to do more than just appear accommodating to what she and her father believed, that is if she really saw me as a man and not just as a potential convert, which unfortunately I was by no means certain of. They would expect me to become fully immersed in their world-view and to make up my mind which side I was on. It wouldn't be good enough just to stand in the sidelines as I had been doing. I would have to join them in their struggle to uphold their beliefs, in effect becoming a different kind of man from the one that I really was.

In their scheme of things there weren't many different kinds of men to choose from. There weren't even three – believers, unbelievers and those who couldn't make up their mind. There were only two. Those who were in, and those who were out. A choice quotation was to them the supreme word of authority on this matter. "He that denies me before men I also will deny before my father who is in Heaven."

One of these two men, I mused, the one who is imbued with the Spirit of the Age, will be searching the heavens with a telescope hoping to find a star which has a planet on which life might exist. If he can detect the presence of water on it he will feel he is on the right track because of the likelihood that life here on earth began in water, in a warm puddle.

This man with the telescope, will be awed by what he sees through it. The universe is so big that he will almost get lost in the vast distances he is able to cover, and in the ones even beyond these that he knows are there. When his friend with the microscope reverses the process and tells him of the not dissimilar wonders that he can see, the man will feel confident that all such things owe their existence to something other than an old-fashioned God who has a particular concern for man and a personal interest in his affairs.

The second of the two men, I continued to suppose, almost but not quite out of my depth in this elevated subject, feels that he doesn't need to look through the telescope, or the microscope, with the same sense of urgency. What he needs to know about the origin of life he thinks has already been revealed to him, although he does have at least one thing in common with the first man. Neither of them, the historical geologists and their opponents among them, can rightly say that science has proved or disproved that there was a great worldwide flood and that Noah and his ark actually existed. The opinion of a scientist is not necessarily any more scientific than the opinion of a layman, as the Pastor was always pointing out. Denying something is not the same as refuting it. Both men believe or disbelieve things they can't prove about things they cannot fully understand.

The trouble was, however, these things, and what went with them, weren't just strongly held opinions to her father. His whole way of life was based on them. To him, history with all its political, religious and moral developments had been made by them, and current events were being shaped by them. Although divine intervention in human affairs was strong stuff, even for someone who owned a Book Collection, I had found it surprisingly easy to pull things out of that very Book Collection in support of some of the national events, which he had attributed to God:

1. Ancient Syria fell, according to the Pastor, because of its barbaric treatment of others.

    And so did at least two present day great nations, Germany and Japan, only seventy odd years ago.

2. Ammon suffered because it attacked another country purely to add to its own possessions.

   And so, too, more recently, did Italy, which invaded Ethiopia in 1935, only to be itself attacked and brought low by Germany some ten years later.

3. Edom, was humbled because it thought itself impregnable and trusted in its own greatness.

   As was present day America, for inclining towards this error, when one of its great cities, New Orleans, was devastated by a flood the humiliating effects of which were heightened by the length of time it took to send help.

That many forms of divine intervention were said by the Pastor to be a warning rather than a final punishment I thought lifted some of the heaviness from his world-view. After all, without a restraining influence of some kind acting on the affairs of men how many great political criminals hell-bent on conquering the world, would have brought about the total destruction of the human race, or reduced mankind to the level of the beast, were it not for that force or that principle which has operated against them throughout history: "Thus far shall you come and no farther, and here shall your proud waves be stayed."

The idea of fully indentifying with the Pastor in his way of life rather than merely subscribing to his beliefs, was another matter, however. Perhaps only a few generations ago these beliefs wouldn't have been so far from the mainstream but now, in holding so strictly to them, he appeared to be an almost cult-like figure. In subscribing to certain basic tenets he was certainly a fundamentalist, if not quite in the derogatory sense the word was being used today. Unfortunately there were many who couldn't see past the label, and in entering into this way of life what would that make me appear to be, too?

Very enthusiastic, but in a balanced and realistic way, he was in no sense a fanatic, always responding to criticism in a gentle and forthright manner. Nor did the Pastor resemble a false teacher whose personal opinions were being cleverly put forward as facts. But he nevertheless had a way of wearing you down. Seemingly aware of what was going on in your mind he would put your own cherished contemporary beliefs under scrutiny and make you doubt their true validity just as you had at first doubted his.

It hadn't taken him long, in the first instance, to persuade me that there was more than a grain of truth in some of his 'outlandish' assertions, and that some of these might well be on an agenda other than that drawn up by modern man.

To say that natural catastrophes, whether brought on by global warming, geological upheavals, or just the weather in general, were sometimes controlled and directed by an unseen hand didn't mean, he was at pains to point out, that he refuted the scientific explanations concerning these things, only that he was suggesting another point of origin and another purpose in certain specific cases – the storm that scattered the Spanish Armada sent against England in 1588, the rain at Waterloo which helped Wellington defeat Napoleon in 1815 and many more events were to him examples of divine intervention, and those who preferred not even to consider this were, according to him, running away from reality or were being driven by their emotions rather than by their intellect.

And if these interventions, or visitations, as the Pastor sometimes called them, concerned nations and the component parts of those nations – men, it didn't seem unreasonable of him to make the point that very few people, when personally threatened by the effect of a great natural disaster, continued to believe that God had nothing to do with it. Rather the opposite, he contended. Such people were often brought to their knees and made to realise how puny and insignificant they were – which, according to him, was one of the reasons these events occurred in the first place. And these people were the lucky ones, he argued – if their experiences made them sit up and think, if they heeded the warning, such as the one associated with the Great Flood.

But the majority of men who were not themselves directly affected by these great disasters, were hardly going to be dumbfounded because a few thousand people had perished in some foreign land during a great convulsion. It was here, therefore, that the Pastor came into his own, as far as I was concerned. He had the ability to make these things into something that affected you personally, regardless of your circumstances, to make you feel that his world-view was the right one, that he was a witness to the fact that not only did divine intervention occur in the affairs of nations and in the affairs of men in general but in your own in particular. And as I had sat there in the car deciding to sever my connection with Andy's people it had really been this, or rather the consequences implicit in disregarding it, that had been the deciding factor.

That I had afterwards changed my mind, and, like mankind in general, had thought at the time I had a very good excuse, didn't alter the fact that I could now see the truth of the matter. No longer was there that great moral ache within me which symptomatically asked questions like the one Job had asked. "Why do bad people prosper?" "They don't", I once more remembered the Pastor saying. "Away with fractional knowledge and selective memory", he had said "and look more closely at the facts. See what happens with the passage of time, even if you can't look into their hearts "right now."

But in spite of all this, wasn't I right to be concerned about how deeply involved I got? In lamenting that I was no stranger to the feeling of not belonging surely my sense of identity was important. What I would look like to other people would be what Linda and the Pastor had first looked like to me. I could hardly leave my image out of it.

The Pastor, in this respect, certainly belied the projected popular image of his Master, who in appearance was often depicted as a gormless looking man with a beard wearing robes like curtains. Instead he had well-chiselled features with the thin lips, sloping forehead and slightly set back eyes of a man of vigour and determination. His rugged features and sturdy build were more like those of a building site foreman than a man of a the cloth and there was a firm friendliness in his manner of speaking that made most people, inside and outside the Church, respectful and passive in their dealings with him. As a person he was someone I myself could like, as well as respect.

Also on the positive side, with regard to the demands all this would make on me was a very surprising and significant fact from the Book Collection. Hadn't Grand Admiral Doenitz, capable head of the German Navy in World War II, on the wrong side, but surely sincerely wrong – his two sons were lost in the same cause – hadn't he in later life attached himself to the same 'Master' as the Pastor had? As had a Japanese pilot who was prominent in the attack on Pearl Harbour. Strange as it may seem, I would be in some quite good company.

*

But where did all these things leave me, right now, with regard to Linda? Was I right in thinking that my relationship with her was inextricably linked to them, or was there a shade of meaning that I had failed to grasp? I began to see that there was.

The true Church was an organism rather than an organisation, the Pastor had once told me, and there was no doubt about where I stood with regard to the two for, rightly or wrongly, I had never been too keen on the organisation, while Linda, in this respect, was exactly the opposite. The Church organisation was her life.

That she was only going to accept me on this basis, I could see now was inevitable and, as I had already concluded, it would take a lot of hard work on my part to bridge a gap of this kind. Was this something I would be able to cope with in such a close personal relationship? Would I end up, if things took their natural course, changing my title to husband while in practice I was still a kind of suitor? Was I forever going to be a supplicant, then? Would there once more be a big desk in my life with me sitting permanently on the wrong side of it. It was this, rather than her actual beliefs themselves, that was the problem. The two were closely related, but I could see at last that it was the nature of our relationship which was bothering me, not the nature of her beliefs. They were two different things.

But there was a serious flaw in my relationship with Karen, too. Getting it wrong about where she stood with Andy had coloured everything I had said to her and had prevented me from even hinting at what I felt about her. I didn't really know where I stood with her now any more than I did with Linda. Had these occasions when our eyes had met, when she had looked at me in that strange way, merely been her response to the situation, not to me?

That I was now beginning to think about her almost in the same way as I had first thought about Linda didn't seem right for I didn't feel the same way about them. This was something that only the night at the flat with Karen had made me realise. Although my feelings for Linda were very strong, they were different in texture from those that had made me that evening, associate Karen with Chopin. The music had enabled me to see something I had been unable to put into words?

In that other world of being, to which had music so often transported me, there were emotions that existed in this world, too. Some of these I could find a name for – tenderness, longing. But there were emotions that came to life only in that other world, and for which I had no name, which gave me the deepest satisfaction. It was these, I saw at last, that were present in the effect that Karen always, and Linda never, had on me. This could mean only one thing, and there was a kind of finality about it.

In an attempt to clear my head I went over to the window and looked out onto the car park. There was no longer the danger of having unwelcome visitors. A great weight had been lifted from my mind. I felt secure in my possession of the money and could indeed look out at the world from a position of strength now. I could, to a much greater extent than before, choose my actions but there was no doubt about it, it still didn't give me the final say in what the result of these actions was going to be. The money wasn't going to solve anything as far as my problems with Linda and Karen were concerned.

In these, I had to find another angle, another way of looking at things, and almost at once I could see that while I was worried so much about the demands Linda might make on me, the only misgivings I had ever had about Karen concerned the relationship I thought she had had with Andy. Any great regret I would feel in parting from Linda would be tempered, however slightly, by the relief I would feel at no longer having to think about the many adjustments I might have to make to my way of life. It would be nothing like this with Karen. Parting from her would only have a down side. There would be a sense of loss attached to it, real loss, and I now knew at this very point, with absolute certainty, that it was her and not Linda that I wanted to be with.

But just as intense and formidable as my feelings were for Karen at this point, were the feelings, of an entirely different kind, that I still had for Linda.

These were feelings that had bothered me since I had first met her and which had now crystallised into a stark realisation of the fact that Linda was too good for me. She outclassed me as a person. The taunt of many a deprived person directed at someone more fortunate – "You think you are better than me" – had been reversed in my view of her. I could have said to her, in all sincerity, "I think you "are" better than me."

Linda represented a kind of undeniable excellence, like that emanating from the scene of a beautiful, winsome young concert pianist playing Chopin on a Steinway – who had shown excellence in her personal qualities, excellence in her ability as a pianist, excellence in her choice of instrument, and excellence in her choice of composer.

So too, as far as I was concerned, did excellence emanate from Linda in her world – a world that I couldn't truly belong in and should never even have tried to.

Linda was definitely far too good for me! Excellent in her personal qualities, excellent in the way she could adhere to, express and emphasize her beliefs, and excellent, even if controversially so, in her choice of creative source material.

What therefore was my next step going to be? Now that the dangers which had brought Karen and me together had passed? What, if anything, did I really mean to her? Was there anything other than wishful thinking to give me hope? Once more, in spite of my aversion to the idea, I would have to become a supplicant, a suitor. But with Karen I wasn't going to shrink from the idea. I couldn't.

And surely the odds weren't altogether stacked against me this time. Of course the money wouldn't decide everything, but it would help. I was nobody's man now.

But how much money in real terms did I actually have?, I asked myself. It certainly covered the full spectrum of my immediate needs. I had moved from insufficiency to sufficiency, almost to abundance. But I hadn't done it alone. The money really wasn't all mine. So how much of it should I actually keep for myself I wondered. I would have to get this clear before I went to the party.

But 'How much should I keep?' didn't seem to be the right question. It sounded much better to ask, 'How much did they deserve?' If there was a way of dividing up the spoils that didn't remind me of the way Sears arrived at his ungenerous rates of commission I was going to find it.

There was Andy, Tom, Karen, Liz and myself to consider. Should I split it five ways?

But Liz hadn't really been in on it, and Tom had only got involved at the last minute.

And yet, what Tom had done had been absolutely crucial. And Liz had always been there for us and would have helped if we had asked her.

As for Karen, she had almost done as much as I had. I started again.

Although the theory and practice of tricking Sears, and quite a few other things, had been down to me alone, none of this would ever have happened without Andy. The bottom line was, Andy had helped me when I really needed it, when there was no one else, and I had done much the same for him. It had to be fifty fifty.

Andy could take care of Tom out of his half and I could take care of Karen out of mine. Karen could take care of Liz.

chapter
twenty-seven

DANCING WITH LIZ WAS CHALLENGING BUT enjoyable, just as it had been at the previous party. It wasn't anything remotely like that with Karen. No matter what I said I couldn't get her to respond in the right way.

Although she seemed relaxed and quite friendly, there was absolutely no trace of the intimacy I had been hoping for.

I was glad when the dance came to an end. Dancing with Liz had been physically exhausting but this particular dance, with Karen, had been a mental and emotional strain, an ordeal almost as intense in its own way as the one I had so recently gone through. As we parted at the end of the dance, she going to the opposite corner of the room, I tried to face the fact that what I feared, concerning my relationship with her, had come to pass. Now that the events which had drawn us together were over, I was finding out where I really stood with her. Nowhere, it would seem.

Andy waved me over. He was beginning to look like his old self again and had been banging his crutch on the floor in time with the music. As I took my seat beside him he propped the crutch up against the wall and leaned over the table towards me.

"Here's something to tide you over John," he said, slipping an envelope to me under the table. "And there's stuff for you at the Casino, too, if you want it. It pays a lot more than you ever got in Bartons. A lot more."

"Actually I don't need the money, Andy," I said hesitantly.

"John, I owe you one," he insisted. "It took a lot of guts to do what you did."

If I wasn't getting things right with Karen, at least I was getting them right with Andy, I felt strongly, in this role reversal. At the previous party it had been me who had been thanking him for the loan, feeling grateful even for his friendship. It was almost the other way round now.

"Andy, I couldn't have got the package back if Karen hadn't gone with me to the caravan, and what would have happened if Big Tom hadn't turned up at the boat? Don't thank me, thank them."

"I'm thanking the whole bloody lot of you, but you first, John."

As I listened to him explain further about his involvement in smoothing the way for the new owners of the Casino, and then about where Sears had fitted in, with his position and influence on various Planning Committees and a good few other things, I realised how lucky I had been to come out of all this unscathed, how much out of my depth I had really been. But it was still Karen who was deciding my mood.

"I warned Sears about using small-time people like Steve," Andy went on. "But he wouldn't listen. He certainly got what was coming to him."

"Actually, he didn't 'get what was coming to him', Andy. Not exactly," I couldn't resist saying.

"He didn't?"

Andy looked puzzled. Once more it was actually me who was setting the pace.

"No. I got what was coming to him," I said.

His puzzled look changed to one of amazement as I explained to him about the money under the freezer. But he didn't say much, remaining silent as I told him how I intended to split it up.

"Are you sure this is what you want to do?" he asked at last, still with a look of bewilderment on his face.

"Well, what else?" I replied.

"John, you're a bloody wonder," he said.

Still feeling low from my encounter with Karen, my spirits rose momentarily at Andy's words. I had almost forgotten where I had started out in all this, right at the very bottom. But here I was, safely on a ladder almost as good as Jacob's. I could forget about the fact that the lack of money was a kind of impotence. And I was no longer a kind of fugitive either. But my spirits sunk again as I thought of Karen.

"I've just been lucky, Andy," I added truthfully, without enthusiasm.

Leaving him to pass on the information about the money to Tom I decided it was time to tell Karen, too. If I needed a reason, as I felt I did, to ask her for another dance, then this was certainly it.

But it was the same again. I had seen the look before, in the Old Toll Bar when I had hardly known her, and in the car when she had suspected me of lying to her about my connection to the Operation.

The unwelcome reserve in her manner could only mean one thing, I supposed. She didn't like me in the right way. She knew what my feelings were for her, and she wasn't going to offer me any encouragement. That explained it. But I couldn't give up. Not just yet.

"Have I said something wrong?" I asked her stupidly, aware that I hadn't said anything at all, yet.

"No. Why?" she asked, looking up at me as if I hadn't said something stupid.

"I'm disappointed in your attitude, that's all."

"My attitude?" She asked, looking puzzled now. "My attitude to what?"

"To me," I told her, deciding it had to be plain speaking from now on. "To the fact that I was mistaken about you and Andy."

"And what exactly did you think my attitude was going to be?" she snapped.

I struggled to find the right words. But if her question was an honest one, and from the look on her face it seemed that it was, then what was the point. It seemed that my doubts had been right all along. I had been hoping for too much. Whatever the bond between us had been, it didn't follow that the feelings we had for each other had to be identical. What other way could she have acted in those last few days, anyway? Of course we had got on well. Of course she seemed to like me. She probably did. She had to, in a situation like that, with people like Steve and the smiling man to contend with, and then the fear that we were being stalked by the Operation.

"You'll go to sleep dancing with him, Karen," Liz cut in, as she jerked and wriggled past us with Big Tom on her arm.

"Cheers, John," Big Tom shouted above the noise, making a thumbs up sign that signified Andy had told him about the money he would be getting.

Like Andy, Tom was important to me. A friend from the

start, boyishly good-natured, yet formidable and threatening with others whenever it was called for. It felt really good to be doing him a favour.

"Cheers big man," I shouted back, returning the thumbs up sign, glad not only that I had earned his respect but also that I had been able to demonstrate my friendship.

But was I just a friend to Karen, too. Was that all. How far wrong about this had I actually been?

"There's something important I have to tell you," I said to her.

"About what?"

"The money."

"What money?"

I searched her features as I told her, hoping the revelation might at least make her soften a little towards me. But she looked less surprised than Andy had been, and not even impressed.

"And that's between Liz and me?" she asked, in a formal tone of voice.

"Give Liz whatever you want."

"Thank you very much," she said, as if I had just given her an uninteresting birthday present.

The dance was coming to an end and she began to look about the room.

"I'd better find Liz and tell her the good news, she said, breaking away from me.

As I watched her go I felt I had to get away from this whole situation, from everything. I had come through all this travail successfully. I was a victor. But because of Karen, I had nothing but the taste of defeat in my mouth.

chapter
twenty-eight

I NO LONGER HAD MY BACK TO THE WALL. I HAD reversed the likely outcome of a devastating set of circumstances. But it didn't seem to matter now. My relationship with Karen had spoiled it all.

On this occasion I wasn't running away, I almost convinced myself, or making a statement. I was merely moving on. It was best to get as far away from her as possible.

As I wondered where this well-trodden pathway might lead, other than to joining the Foreign Legion, I had to admit that it had never occurred to me up to that point that Aunt Bethea might be able to provide me with an answer of some kind. The reason I had come to see my great aunt, on this particular occasion, still wasn't too clear to me.

I knew it was unlikely she would have much more of immediate interest to tell me about my father, my grandfather, or my great grandfather. She had already told me so much. But finding out that behind the scenes she had often been active in my behalf, and had, contrary to what I had been led to believe, considered me to be part of the family had awakened in me a sense of belonging, to her as well as to my Aunt Grace. I wanted to clarify the effect that the events of the last few weeks had had on me in the light of this. I wanted to get my feet back on the ground, to decide in which direction I was meant to go, without Karen, unfortunately.

As I sat across from my great aunt, unhindered by the debasing need for financial help, and feeling quite entitled to be there, I at first misunderstood the reason for her thoughtfulness. She was about to say something about fire extinguishers, or an oil painting, or a distant family relative, I supposed.

"You weren't happy at the Food Importers?" she asked instead.

The question shouldn't have affected me the way that it did. After all, I now knew that it was her who had got me the job there in the first place. But it was the worst thing she could have asked me. How could I explain why I had left without lowering her opinion of me? I couldn't' lie to her. Perhaps she even knew already. What had happened in the ante room at the Annual Staff Dance was something I wanted to forget about. The part I had played in my recent problems showed me up in a very poor light indeed, and it might look even worse than that to her.

"The work there was fine," I told her, deciding to feel my way.

"But you prefer working with fire extinguishers?" she returned.

"I don't actually," I had to say. How could I say otherwise.

"I've been in touch with your old boss," she told me, taking me completely by surprise.

"The young one?" I asked at once. I loved the interest she

was taking in my plight, but had she got to the bad part about the events in the ante room? I wondered feverishly.

"No, his father," she told me.

Did it really matter? Everyone in there would know the story, anyway. But it did matter.

"He thinks very highly of you."

"That's good to know," I returned, trying not to show how relieved I felt that the incident in the ante room didn't appear to have come up.

"He was telling me his son has settled down now and that they both regret that you left in the way that you did."

"They do?" I gulped, again taken completely by surprise.

But I rallied quickly as I guessed what she was about to tell me. What would once have seemed ridiculous now seemed interesting, even possible.

"They want you to go back," she said snappily. "What do you think of that, and there will be a promotion in it for you."

"Did he explain why I left?" I asked, no longer so anxious about this but not yet sure how exactly to respond.

"It seems you have a temper," she said, smiling gently.

"Is that what they told you?" I asked, pretending to be indignant so that I would have more time to think.

But I didn't need more time. I was fooling myself. I could go back, because I didn't need to. But I was still fooling myself.

I would go back, mainly at that point, because of Karen. Without her, my destination seemed unimportant.

chapter
twenty-nine

THE WALTZES OF CHOPIN WERE SO VARIED IN effect that one of them would be bound to reflect my mood, I felt, as I pressed the button on the CD player.

But what was my mood? I had to ask myself. I wished it was the euphoria I had experienced on the boat when I knew the money below the freezer was mine and that I had achieved my various objectives.

It had been great feeling that the pressure was off, that my worst fears hadn't come to pass, that I had been able to keep going and come through all this. If only it felt that way now.

Since the waltzes, to my great disappointment, didn't take me anywhere near the higher world of knowledge or being, my thoughts turned to the picture on the wall of the Sales Office. I found that I could remember it clearly enough for my purpose. I wanted to walk along the depicted riverbank, as I had done so often in the past, and find a place to sit and take stock of the situation.

I was going back to the Food Importers, back to where I had started. In a sense I was going back to where everyone else was, to an ordinary everyday existence, with sufficient money to pay for shelter, food and clothing and sufficient free time to indulge myself, perhaps more than ever now, in my Book Collection.

But would I be the same person? Could I be, after all that had happened?

At first I thought the answer had to be 'yes', for I was now characteristically thinking about Karen, as I had once thought about Linda. Instead of giving my attention to more important matters I was brooding on the fact that she was out of my reach. For a while she was all I could think about. I would miss Andy and the others but it would be much more than that with her. There would be something missing from my world, as well as from the picture.

But what were the other more important matters I should be thinking of? I asked myself. Settling back into the Food Importers and into my old way of life wasn't really one of them, as it should have been. I felt confident, after working for someone like Sears, that I would be able to settle my differences with the new boss. If he had changed, and I knew, as a result of recent experiences that I had, then the incident in the ante-room at the Annual Staff Dance would surely be something we could put behind us. We had both been at fault, and the fact that he wanted me to come back was something I felt neither of us were going to regret. After cold calling on shops I was going to be filled with a new enthusiasm for my old job, particularly now, when I knew I had an Aunt in high places, and the future looked bright.

Perhaps it was important that I concentrate my attention on the things I had learned during the events of these last few weeks. It would be hard to do this without the help of the Book

Collection, I realised, although the books were no substitute for the harsh way in which I had found out what the world outside was really like. It had taken a first hand experience of deceit, despair and determination to do that. But the Books, nevertheless, continued to shed light of a kind.

In the Book Collection there were people I admired, and people I felt I could sit in judgement of. There were heroes and villains. But could I now ask myself which of these I had been when events had challenged me as they had been challenged? Although I had won my war, my little war, I knew the answer wouldn't be flattering.

I had been able to flit in and out of my moral dilemmas with comparative ease. The right thing to do had always ended up being what I felt I had to do, and I knew that if events had taken a turn for the worse I would have progressed yet further in my criminality. What had started out as a mere attempt to augment my income, albeit by dubious means, had almost ended up in murder, and yet even with the benefit of hindsight I had almost persuaded myself that most of what I had done had been right. Apart from my initial mistake in leaving the Food Importers, I thought that none of what had happened afterwards had really been my fault. I had been carried along by events and forced to go in a certain direction even after I had had second thoughts about where it might lead me. But how many of these people in the Book Collection had sincerely thought, and in many cases had actually pleaded, that they had had the same excuse?

In using the Book Collection, in the way that I did, to magnify, to enrich, even to dramatise the relatively mundane events of my life had I stumbled upon something? Wasn't the excuse that I was using to justify my actions the one that mankind in general used? For if so, and everyone thought that his war was a just war, that his problems weren't his fault, and that necessity decided what was right and what was wrong then it was easy to see how even mass murder could be justified, by good men dropping the atom bomb, as well as evil men exterminating people.

Perhaps this was what I should be concentrating on, the fact that I couldn't see how mankind had the ability to make it on its own. This is what I seemed to have learned from my experiences. Mankind was heading for trouble.

I had been heading for trouble, too, but I had got away with it this time. Could I count it as a warning? But mankind has had its warnings, too, as the Pastor pointed out so well. Even my Aunt Grace seemed to know this, with the severity of her less well-defined famines and floods, and her earthquakes of increasing intensity that she was always telling me about.

I wished I could see it all as clearly as the Pastor did. But then, as he had pointed out, the spirit that had gathered together and revealed these truths, upon which so much depended, could conceal their meaning, too.

How much had been concealed from me, I asked myself. Or more importantly, how much had been revealed to me. I had certainly had a glimpse of the kind of destination I had been headed for.

It was the same one that men in general were headed for, men who could look askance at the description of a man given in a book, because it was made up of copies of copies and yet could have blind faith in the existence in a puddle of water millions of years ago of the substances and conditions that would cause life, men who would stake all their beliefs, or their lack of them, on this.

But why could I see where it was all heading if they couldn't? I certainly didn't know why, but I thought I knew how.

I was there, in the Book Collection, with the American marines fighting the Japanese in the 2nd World War. Would the water level over the reef they would have to cross on their assault on the island of Tarawa be deep enough? Most of the people who had lived in that area said that it would be five feet at high tide. Admiral Hill, the man in charge, enquired of any ships' pilots present who had ever been at Tarawa if they could remember any occasions when boats had been unable to cross the reef at high tide? None of them could.

But an old retired soldier who had lived on Tarawa at that time had strongly disagreed.

"You won't have three feet," he had stated categorically during the discussions. And "You definitely won't be able to cross that reef," he had stated with equal vigour at the end of them. But no one had listened to him.

Many things had gone wrong at Tarawa but it was the shallow water over the reef which had claimed the most lives. The marines forced to get out of their boats and wade ashore had been slaughtered. The old resident, the owner of the lone voice, had been right.

Had another lone voice, the voice of Pastor Mackenzie, been right too? In a sense, I could try to forget his daughter Linda, but I could never forget much of what he had said to me concerning certain great truths that mankind had disastrously denied but can never refute.

chapter
thirty

I DIDN'T HAVE TO WAIT LONG OUTSIDE THE OLD Toll Bar. She drew in quite near to me and as she got out I opened the car window in preparation for the ordeal.

I was going against my better judgement in coming here but I couldn't help myself. She now occupied a permanent place in what I remembered of the picture on the sales office wall. I couldn't listen to Chopin without thinking about her, either.

"Karen," I almost trumpeted

As she came over I thought she looked as enticing as she had that day on the beach, the day she had stumbled in the water. It made me feel foolish. Why couldn't I accept the fact that she too was out of my class? But at the same time it encouraged me, as I remembered the way she had looked at me that day on the beach, as I had helped her to her feet.

"John," was all she said as she came over.

"Could I have a word with you, Karen?"

As she got into the car I felt foolish again. What good reason did I have for inviting her into the car to discuss what I merely wished, rather than felt, existed between us?

But I would have to go ahead with it now.

"I've got my old job back, Karen," I told her. "I've just come to say goodbye."

I had an idea what her response was going to be. It wasn't going to be overwhelming.

"I hope everything goes all right for you," she said, just as I had expected.

The Karen of my dreams had definitely gone forever, I could see, wishing that I hadn't come.

"I can't say I'm surprised you're going, John," she said, opening the car door to get out only minutes after she had got in. "You don't really belong here, do you," she added.

There was an iciness in her tone that compelled me to answer. She might want rid of me but she didn't have to overdo it.

"I don't belong?" I asked indignantly. After all that has happened?"

"I didn't mean it in that way. How could I," she said in an apologetic tone that I hadn't expected.

"Well, in what way?"

To my surprise she settled back down in her seat again and turned to face me.

"I suppose I'm just not used to people who own original oil paintings with their name on them."

"What's that got to do with anything?" I protested, and anyway I thought you liked the painting," I added hopelessly.

"It's not just that. What about all this religion and Chopin?"

"What religion?"

I saw at once what she meant. It was even worse than I had thought. This was how I had been coming over to her. I was a kind of upgraded wimp, which would more or less finish the matter once and for all.

"Well, that girl you told me about," she went on. "She's religious isn't she?"

"Linda?"

"Yes her. It's to be you and me in the pub and you and Linda in the pew. Is that it?"

'You and me'. Had the Karen I loved reappeared, if only to taunt me?

"You're too much for me, John. It's just as well you're going away."

It was the way that she said it. Had I just been thrown a lifeline right at the very last minute?

"Too much? In what way?"

"You come across as though you're too good for all this and the next minute you're behaving like a criminal, beating these people at their own game. And now you have all this money. My God, John, who are you?"

I loved this. The Karen of my dreams had definitely reappeared. How was she to know that desperation had played as big a part in all this as had determination? All she could have seen was what I had let her see and hadn't I been careful in acting the part, anxious to look good in front of her? I had very nearly talked myself out of something.

"I was lucky Karen. That's all."

"Lucky to the tune of £100,000, John? Do me a favour."

"Karen, you've got me all wrong. You've completely misunderstood me."

"Well, who are you, John? Tell me."

"An unemployed ex-fire extinguisher salesman," I said bluntly. "But I've had the offer of a job, as I've just told you."

That she would prefer me in this lowly capacity was something I hadn't even considered. When I finally told her about Aunt Grace, and the Foot Importers, about Linda, about the oil painting and Aunt Bethea, I was overwhelmed by the change that came over her. She was back! Karen was back!

"I know you won't believe me, John," she said later. "But I actually like Chopin very much."

"I don't really care if you do or not," I replied, pushing my idol into second place where he belonged now. She was looking at me, wide-eyed, as she had done crouched down behind the bushes outside the caravan. Karen was back to stay.